THE BODY
OF THE BEASTS

THE BODY
OF THE BEASTS

AUDRÉE WILHELMY

TRANSLATED BY SUSAN OURIOU

ARACHNIDE

First published as *Le corps des bêtes* in 2017 by Leméac Éditeur Inc.
First published in English in Canada and the USA in 2019
by House of Anansi Press Inc.

www.houseofanansi.com

23 22 21 20 19   1 2 3 4 5

Library and Archives Canada Cataloguing in Publication

Title: The body of the beasts / Audrée Wilhelmy ; translated by Susan Ouriou.
Other titles: Corps des bêtes. English
Names: Wilhelmy, Audrée, 1985– | Ouriou, Susan, translator.
Description: Translation of: Le corps des bêtes.
Identifiers: Canadiana (print) 20189053178 | Canadiana (ebook) 20189053186
| ISBN 9781487006105 (softcover) | ISBN 9781487006112 (EPUB)
| ISBN 9781487006129 (Kindle)
Classification: LCC PS8645 I432 C6713 2019 | DDC C843/.6—dc23

Library of Congress Control Number: 2018962106

Book design: Alysia Shewchuk

 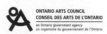

We acknowledge for their financial support of our publishing program
the Canada Council for the Arts, the Ontario Arts Council, and the Government
of Canada. We acknowledge the financial support of the Government of Canada
through the National Translation Program for Book Publishing, an initiative of the
Roadmap for Canada's Official Languages 2013–2019: Education, Immigration,
Communities, *for our translation activities.*

Printed and bound in Canada

To Simon, Jean, Colombe, Rose-Anne—
the sturdy boughs on which our own branches grow.

your silence will be everywhere and in the same way
everything hushed here speaks of you i believe
i'll find you before nightfall i look for pebbles
in my pockets with each cry or creaking
of the wood which is you in your entirety

Alexie Morin

Mie is doing it again. She scrunches up her mind and imagines herself tugging on a string so its matter emerges from her ear and shimmers before her, malleable as a scrap of fabric; she rolls it up tight and slides it into the brain of another, that of a fish soon to perish, an ant, or one of the great stags braying on the edge of the forest.

She is lying on the bed. Her twelve-year-old shape shows beneath the sheet: even covered, she feels exposed. She has no idea how to tame her nakedness, it's a sort of animal inside which her mind is incapable of penetrating. So she grasps a morsel of her consciousness and thrusts it into the skull of the great blue heron alighting on the window ledge, she clucks her tongue against the roof of her mouth and it takes off, all long legs and greyish-blue feathers, above the coast.

She gains altitude with the bird. She rises above the lighthouse, sees the rocks of the craggy foreshore appearing like an army beneath the waves, the bands of golden sand, the seaweed and crabs teeming underneath, the lagoon; she spots Seth and Abel, minuscule from on high, lining up hare carcasses on a pyre of rocks and branches, and, beside the Old Woman, little Dé turning wet sand into mud pies. Farther along the strand: the dilapidated cabin, its chiming shells, the collection of dried starfish on the steps to the porch, its broken railing. From the sky, Mie can see the thatched roof, mould-blackened and perforated again. Fresh tracks plough the earth — a woman's steps have traced a straight line between the dunes and the cabin. Her mother hides inside, draws maps and trails on the cabin walls, fragments of forests, towns, countries. She conjures creatures and children. Mie would like to linger nearby but the bird does not stop; it soars to the trees crowning the cliffs, lands on top of a beech, and takes flight again — perhaps it will travel as far as Seiche and feast on deep-sea fish snatched from trawlers — then it flies out of reach, disappears.

The sheet is cold against her hard nipples, her belly, and her pubescent mound. Spiked hairs cling to the fabric. In a flash, Mie's thoughts return to her own body. She is naked. No other creature is in sight. She is alone.

I

A wharf jutting out into the open sea. Waves rumble below, foam spouts from cracks between the planks. Men angle for tuna and stingrays. They cast their lines from the platform at the far end of the jetty, where the water is already deep, and wrest huge creatures from the sea that drench them in salt water as they writhe in mid-air and then again on the pier's wooden planking. A warm breeze blows in from the interior and whips the clothing of passersby against their bodies and roars in their ears. Perched on the guardrails or on the backs of benches, children eat ice cream that trickles between their fingers and onto their bare bellies. The heat of the beach is like no other, worn like a piece of clothing.

So different from the others in their long shirts, the Borya brothers serve as their mother's bodyguards. She holds the youngest on her hip and strides toward the fishermen, her skirts billowing around her legs. Three coins jangle in her pocket and their clinking combines with the clacking of her heels against the wharf. The biggest fish require tough bargaining, so the boys' father sent his wife. He told her to wear her grey dress, the one with the low-cut square neck that shows off her breasts, plump with milk. She makes her way toward the men, her attempt at sensuality somewhat hindered by the presence of her sons. The eldest walks in front of her, pushing a wheelbarrow three times his weight to transport the animal once the deal has been made. The younger two run to keep up with their mother's swaying gait. As for her, she sees only the huge fish hanging mid-wharf, the fishermen's sturdy bodies, the blue water and the light sparkling on its surface.

Osip Borya, chasing a salamander, has stayed behind. By the time he loses the tiny creature in the tall grasses, his mother and brothers have left. He can't see them anywhere. Immediately overhead, seagulls wheel like sparrow hawks. A pelican swoops toward the beach, throat stretched taut with its catch, and lands on a post right next to the boy. The bird is still dripping from its plunge into the water. It looks at the child, throws its skull back and, swallowing its prey in one majestic gulp, unfurls its wings. At that exact moment, several things occur. First, the pelican lifts off and returns to its position on the waves. Then, watching the seabird, Osip spies his mother at the end of the wharf and notices a tiny movement she makes:

as her right foot lifts out of its shoe, she reaches down to brush sand off the sole of her foot. Just behind her, a fisherman lets out a shout and hauls from the water a five-foot-long swordfish thrashing around like a demon. Three men harpoon it to sap the creature's strength.

Osip memorizes it all. The curly down on the pelican's neck, the pearls of water on its feathers, the extended pouch below its beak, the exact shape of the still-living fish sliding down its esophagus from throat to gizzard, the silence of the prey's extinction amid the continuous din of the beach; his mother's tanned hand brushing her white foot, the ankle he'd never noticed before, her bosom as she reaches down; the raised bill of the swordfish, its death throes, the light striking the metal tips of the harpoons, the blood mingling with the salt water spilling into the sea and along the dock, gently splashing his mother's dress and brown hand though not her foot, already tucked back beneath her underskirt.

Suddenly, Osip's small sex stiffens. There's no controlling the phenomenon: the rod rises, a stranger to the child. A secret part of his body has come to life and suddenly the fear of being found out by his brothers, by the fishermen — grown men — washes over him.

He sinks into the tall grasses and waits for the stiffness to pass. It takes forever. His mother is still visible;

from afar, he recognizes her dress and her braids. He knows he must avert his eyes because if not — it has taken him a while to understand as much — his sex will never soften. He looks for something to distract him: a shell, a crab. Occasionally, intense concentration on a jellyfish — a medusa — restores some suppleness to his member. He catches sight of the salamander he tracked earlier and meets its black gaze. It has two yellow spots on its eyelids and he focuses all his energy there. He tries to shake off the thought of his mother's ankle by studying the salamander's skull, but its ocelli call to mind the circles of his mother's breasts. He has to find a way to rid himself of thoughts of her. His mother. Her tanned wrist and the bounce to her chest, restrained by her undergarments, when she brushes her hair, when she eats, when she carries the baby on her hip.

He tugs at his pants, backs deeper into the bushes. He glances up at the dock, ever so briefly, so as not to look at his mother yet see her all the same. He strokes his member, just below its unsheathed head. His mother haggles, she moves her body like a woman of the street, swaying her hips as she measures the size of the swordfish. She sets the youngest down on the bench and ruffles the eldest's hair.

At precisely this moment in his life, Osip Borya is mindful of four certainties:

1. His eldest brother is no longer a virgin.
2. His mother has done him the Great Favour.
3. Osip, too, will have his turn. (But when?)
4. He is ready.

Fifteen years later, the eldest brother's woman makes the same gesture. Osip sees her from the lighthouse observation gallery: she raises her foot and brushes the sole with her hand, a trifling act that shouldn't arouse him yet still gives him pause. He's not met her yet, she's only just arrived, brought out of the forest by Sevastian-Benedikt along with a half-dozen hares for skinning. She holds her dress against her knees; its train drags in the sea like a dead animal. A puffed sleeve has slipped down her arm. Her shoulder is exposed to the sun, the top of the dress loose across her belly and her slim throat visible at the neckline. The lower part of the dress sticks to her thighs: no bustle, underskirt, or form, nothing but the frayed fabric against her skin.

Since the Boryas left Seiche for Sitjaq and its lighthouse, the only woman that Osip — nineteen, chief lantern keeper — has ever known is his mother. The stranger troubles him. She's older than he is and so free, behaves like a wild child — she walks barefoot, her heels scar the sand, she eats fish and rice with her fingers, tears her dresses and doesn't mend them. For the past fortnight, she's not spoken a word, though she has often sung in a language of harsh accents. She has an erratic way of filling the hours, spends her days on futile tasks. Here she is, for instance, carrying pails out to the waves. She fills them with medusas washed up onto the shore, then piles the jellyfish in the shade of the beech trees crowding the cabin. She holds her chin high as she walks, her head tipped back slightly as though the bun in her hair weighs heavy on the nape of her neck, which extends in a long line from her shoulder blades. The neckline of her dress rides low, droops, and exposes her breasts. It is an ensemble that both conceals and reveals her body, and Osip has never seen anything like it.

A child's heated emotion. The stranger bends down to extract a shell lodged between her toes, revealing both her décolleté and her ankles. His sex thickens and presses up against the seam of his clothing. Neither the Old Woman nor his eldest brother is in sight. Only the new arrival occupies the beach; she walks, and water from the pails splashes over the bottom of her dress, its fabric hugging her legs. Osip leans back against the lighthouse, wishing the stone would swallow him whole, wishing he were able to disappear till he was nothing but two eyes and a phallus. He undoes his trousers and uncoils his penis, thumb and index finger closed around its flesh; he no longer strokes but tugs at it, his movements quick, his breathing and his pleasure too. He wipes his hand on his trousers, then returns to the lantern. All day long, he lurks on the gallery and spies on the stranger.

Before moving to Sitjaq's rugged terrain, an eight-hour walk from Seiche, the Borya father, mother, and five sons live in a shack, where they eke out a living curing fish caught on the high seas. Everything in the shack is secured by something else; furniture remains standing thanks to the support of the walls and rocks. Aside from the parents' room, big enough for a bed and a dresser, there are two bedrooms in the house, divvied up unequally between the brothers. Osip and Leander share their parents' old mattress, laboriously stuffed into a frame far too small. Matvey and Golby sleep in a chest of drawers leaning against the living room partition. The top and bottom drawers are filled with wadding and once served as cradles; much time has passed yet the little ones have still not been relocated elsewhere, and now their legs and arms dangle and their heads extend beyond the sides of the drawers. Sevastian-Benedikt has the attic to himself and enters it through a trap door. Every night, he has to stand on a chair and hoist himself up; at the crack of dawn he drops to the kitchen floor and his heavy landing awakens everyone else.

There is no window in the garret. Heads have to be bowed to avoid bumping into its frame. Light filters between the beams. Even in winter, the wind that penetrates the walls is not enough to cool the attic since the stovepipe rises through the middle. Sometimes, when the house is empty, Osip climbs up into the attic and takes in every detail: its expanse to begin with, its smells, and his oldest brother's treasures. One day, in a bold moment, he stretches out on the mattress. It buckles beneath him and he realizes the shape left by his weight won't be the same as that left by Sevastian, so he jumps to his feet, beats the straw pallet, and smooths the blanket. Doing this makes the floor creak. At night, Osip hears his brother Sevastian-Benedikt turn over in his sleep; the floor doesn't creak in quite the same way when he reads, dreams, or touches himself.

Below, the front door slams. Osip freezes. He's not allowed in his brother's room. From the far end of the kitchen come loud scraping noises. He turns, careful not to make the floorboards creak, and nudges open the trap door a crack. His mother has dragged the large basin over to the stove and is boiling water: steam rises from the kettle and the pots. A few years back, when he was six or seven, Osip would sit by his mother's side whenever she decided to have a bath, keeping an eye on the babies. He said little and would stare at her glistening legs dangling outside the basin. The soft down on her calves and thighs formed captivating landscapes; he'd imagine himself an explorer bent on discovering the unfamiliar horizons there.

Through the opening, Osip contemplates his mother, her body deformed by the water. She removes a bar of soap from its packaging, wets it, and lathers it between her fingers. She scrubs herself, then sponges off and puts the soap away like a precious object. Osip has never before experienced a scent so refined. He imagines the fragrance wafting up in pink plumes from the washtub to the attic. He's lying on his stomach, the crack through which he observes his mother bathing not quite as wide as his eye. With his face pressed to the crack, he begins to rock his pelvis imperceptibly against the floor, fingers wrapped around his penis, fist against his belly. His mother steps out of the basin; he catches sight of her plump buttocks and arms, nothing more. She grabs a towel, wraps it around herself, then rubs her body with the leftover oil she saves in a small flask after each of their meals. Her hands slide over her limbs and stroke the hair on her body, each trace a new world. Above all she mustn't hear him, Osip prays the floor won't creak. His mother's nails leave marks on her pink skin, and

Osip focuses on the distribution of his weight so his back-and-forth motion doesn't give away his presence; now his mother's palms pass along the long plane of her foot, the curve of her calf, run up her thigh and brush her groin, draw close to her sex, reach her hip, then find the slope of her leg again, down the back this time, stroking her knee, her ankle, her heel. A shudder: something warm trickles between Osip's fingers. He's taken unawares. This has never happened before. He'd like to take a closer look but doesn't dare sit up, he'd make too much noise. In the kitchen, his mother hums as she braids her hair. He rolls onto his back. At the end of his glans is a thin filament that he pulls and pulls. The skinny, sticky cord keeps on coming. This time, his fear of discovery is tinged with newfound pride. His cheeks burn. If only his mother would return to brining her fish. She stays put. He decides to wind the filament around the handle of the trap door, then wipes his fingers on his trousers. He lies there for the longest time. Most likely he dozes off, marvelling at what he's capable of, dreaming of girls in braids, too many to count and all identical to his mother. When he wakes up, the basin has been stored away, his mother has disappeared, and his sperm has dried.

He manages to get back down before Sevastian-Benedikt reappears. He drops into the kitchen and, as he does so, aims a few kicks at the pots to mask the sound of his landing. When it comes to hiding, no one is more gifted than he.

Osip loathes his childhood home as much as he does his life of poverty and his eldest brother's strength. It's impossible to breathe; the shack is too small, too full. For him, it means living outside and venturing inside only for food and sleep. During the day, Sevastian-Benedikt roams the forest, the river, and its mouth, so Osip avoids those areas. He walks the scenic lanes bordering the sea on the far side of Seiche. People from the Cité holiday there. In October, the villas are deserted and lie empty until the buds blossom in late April. Osip glues his nose to the villas' windows and peers at what's inside — furniture draped in sheets, dust floating in rays of sunshine. He wishes he had the audacity to choose a property and winter in it like a cave. He doesn't dare.

One evening, he breaks a window pane, slides his hand through, unbolts a small door to a service entrance, and pushes it open without crossing the threshold. The silence is so heavy it seems to have a sound of its own; the still air smells of lemon oil and scrubbed wood. He stays long enough to take one luxurious breath of it, nothing more. Blood pounds in his temples and he runs away. Later, he can't remember if he shut the door behind him. He imagines bookcases and armchairs infested by vermin because of what he's done. Until the Boryas leave Seiche, he steers clear of that villa. The detour, sticking to the streets instead of the shore, takes twenty minutes.

The more time he spends loitering around fine houses, the more the family's shack disgusts him. The stench of smoked fish clinging to its walls, the living room and kitchen cluttered with mussels, brine, packing, hunting and sewing gear, bags of sugar and salt.

Between the ages of seven and thirteen, as soon as he has finished his breakfast, he heads outside.

One morning, he makes his way to the little bridge and the train station. Leander and he have plans to escape. Every night, wedged together in the hollow in the middle of the mattress, they talk of fleeing to the Cité. Beneath the bed: coins painstakingly amassed, enough to pay for a one-way ticket to the big town. The day before, Leander had asked him again to check the train schedule on the platform's posters.

The trails are covered in ice. Osip slips and slides in his boots. The wind glances off the sea and surges along the path, a gust strews garbage from the tavern, rocking the overhead cables and the pigeons perched there. Lit from behind, the birds swaying on the wire form shadowy shapes still fat with the grain they devoured into November. Osip unbuttons his coat, pulls out a slingshot.

Sevastian-Benedikt hunts with a snare. Some evenings, he'll deposit two or three hares on the table. Their father skins them and washes the pelts, then carves up the carcasses over a wide, shallow pail; their blood and entrails drop into the basin to be thrown into a pit behind the house later on. Their mother makes rabbit pie from the meat, sells the kidneys to the butcher and, with the fur, makes mittens, hats, and collars that their father sells in the Cité, along with the smoked fish. If Osip should bring home a few rock doves, the way his brother does small game, his parents will know what to do. His mother will bake tourtières and sell them at the market; she could stuff her flat pillow with the feathers.

The path is deserted. Osip takes a deep breath. He aims at a pigeon. When it hits the ice, the dull, muffled thud of the fallen bird takes him by surprise. When his stone hit its target, there'd been no cry, no final coo rang out, nothing hinted at death. *Poc.* Nothing more. Overhead, the survivors don't even flinch.

Osip stares at the animal. Ash-grey down on its crop, one wing unfurled, the other tight against its body. Rigid shanks, stiff claws; the neck, rump, beak. When, two years earlier, a partridge hit their window, dust from its plumage left the exact imprint of its death on the glass. This time, nothing. Only a bird once on a wire now lying on the ground, where not even a hollow shows in the path's tamped-down snow. Osip has never killed before. Above him, a dozen quarry bob up and down, oblivious. He yells, he waves his arms; the pigeons don't budge. So he picks up more stones and aims at each of them in turn. They fall without taking flight, without fear.

On the path, thirteen rock doves.

Osip shivers. He's annoyed at the stupidity of their refusal to flee. He still has to pick up their bodies, take them to his father. He draws near, reaches out, his head pulled back. His fingers close around soft, warm feathers. Beneath his palm, the pigeon's flank rises and falls, its breast still beating. Osip recoils, loses his footing, slips on the snow. The pigeon lies a metre away. He should finish it off but he can't. He vomits grey bread from breakfast between his legs.

He wanders off, the birds stay put; they'll freeze beneath the build-up of ice on the street. In the spring, other children will carry them to their parents in houses less shabby than his own.

The train reaches the Seiche terminus at eleven and leaves again two hours later. The whistle sounds, the locomotive chugs and squeals along the rails, white smoke fills the air. Osip holds the railway schedule; he knows the name of each station, the ones with train service and the others that will flash past the windows as the engineer spurs the engine on. He imagines the different stops, the first ones so splendid in the coastal sunshine, but then, before reaching the Cité, Korgata's two stations, Sa-Ann, and after, the papermakers' industrial zone, sad, grey, and packed. He imagines the big city at journey's end, its central station admired by all. In engravings in newspapers, he's seen the flower-decked handrail up the station's main staircase, the mosaics in the lobby, the great glass roof, the impeccable uniforms of the ticket collectors.

The trip from the Seiche station to the Cité terminus takes thirteen hours.

Leander sticks by the window, pokes his head outside, waves and waves. Osip watches the train pull away. He could run behind but stays put on the platform. His brother's fingers recede into the distance and disappear; eventually the train itself vanishes. Osip doesn't budge. He holds the railroad schedule and his own ticket for the Cité tight in his fist. He has squeezed them so hard they form a compact ball good for only one thing—to be thrown on the track.

The first time, the expedition from the Seiche shack to the lighthouse takes six days because all the furniture, fishing gear, clothing, and smaller possessions dear to the brothers and their mother must be ferried through the forest's dense trees and vegetation. Their father doesn't yet know which paths link the village to the open sea—he gets lost two or three times, often wandering blindly, his boys shouldering the entire contents of their household first this way, then that. The trees are massive and tall, even the eldest can't climb their trunks, and their dense foliage hides the stars. All they can do is advance, hoping to find the lighthouse by following the sketchy map they'd been provided with in Seiche. Their mother complains and their father has barricaded himself behind an intimidating silence; he has no idea how he'll lead his brood to safety. Sevastian-Benedikt comes and goes at will, bringing back pheasants and hares that he cooks over fires he builds from twigs and leaves.

Pride drives their father for four days. After that,

he pulls the eldest aside and asks him to find the lighthouse, then sits on the upside-down dresser and watches his son dive in among the tree trunks and tall ferns. Osip has never seen his father like this, slumped over, his chin dropped to his chest. Even their mother doesn't approach him; she sheds tears at the thought that Leander might come upon their empty home should he return from the Cité, and spends the rest of the time with her youngest sons. They fashion spears without the slightest idea how to use them. Osip wishes he could feed his family but can't. When he imagines hunting he's reminded of the pigeons, and whenever he roams through the woods in search of berries, he never recognizes the edible ones and is afraid he'll poison everyone. So he waits. The eldest reappears the next afternoon. He's carrying a lantern and the spyglass from the lighthouse. Fifteen hours later, Osip drops a steamer trunk and a chair on the shore; he walks toward the sea, wades in, lets himself sink into the waves. Thighs, back, head: foam washes over his limbs. Not long after, he sits up and looks at this new territory—vast, deserted, and to be shared with his brothers.

The lighthouse sits on a rock surrounded by reefs. Its imposing structure is connected to the beach by a stone path. The surf has studded it with coral, shells, and mossy seaweed that are revealed at low tide. As the water rises, it swallows up the foreshore and the tower's foundation, breakers crashing and hammering against the stone. Round in design, the bottom third of the lighthouse is built of porous chiselled rubble encircled by a wall that protects the columns, portico, and railing from the violence of heavy seas. Above, the white paint on the watchtower has deteriorated over the years, the matte yellow of brick shows under the flaking coat of paint: a weathered observatory, its windows opening onto the waves, the shore, the forest. Then, higher up, invisible in the sun: the watch gallery, the wire-meshed red lantern, and the verdigris dome mark the horizon. Along the wall and invisible from shore is the huge foghorn that flares out to the open sea and its ships.

Osip has never seen anything this big.

Sitjaq's beach is chalky and speckled in parts with black sand whose patterns shift in the wind. The dunes go on forever, wild around the edges; in the distance, toward Seiche, cliffs pierced with caves hem in the rest. At the edge of the strand, trees sprout suddenly, packed stiff and tight behind a small cabin of wooden planks.

Weary and wet, Osip gets to his feet. He wants to be the first to choose a bed, he checks on his brothers lolling in the surf and drags himself over to their quarters.

The furniture that used to belong to the previous owner is draped in white sheets. Every drawer and closet had been meticulously emptied before their father, Lousbec Borya, was given access. Osip likes the small cabin immediately; its scent of oiled wood, its dust and drapings remind him of the villas in Seiche. He doesn't notice the fungus along the walls or the cracks in the ceiling. He trembles as he removes linen from the bookcases. He'd like to be the only one to pull on the corner of each sheet and reveal a couch, a dresser, a table, but his younger brothers have followed him inside and start throwing the covers off everywhere. Within a minute of their arrival all the furniture is bared, and before Osip is able to commandeer the bunk by the window, they've already staked a claim to it with their bags and returned outside to explore the caves and lagoons.

Passing ships are equipped with masts or propellers; they've come from afar, have crossed the ocean. The names painted on the ships' hulls speak of an unimaginable elsewhere; they're either made of wood or enveloped in grey and red sheathing, except for the trawlers that, in motley colours, look like so many candies bobbing out on the waves. Osip climbs to the lantern every day to study the comings and goings of the commercial, military, and pleasure flotillas. Every morning, he relieves his father; the old man returns to his wife and Osip stays up top. He watches the sea swell and flood the path linking the lighthouse to the shore; he lets the tide rush in and waits for its retreat, listening to the collision of surf and stone. Huge breakers crash against the lighthouse and explode in white spray. Osip, severed from his brothers' world, sits on the gallery, his skin dry from the wind and salt. He counts the ships in the distance, the bow appearing first, then the whole vessel. He logs the date of their approach and then that of their return to the ocean in a notebook. Sometimes, ships' captains make out his silhouette against the flaking paint and sound their big horn; in a single bound Osip leaps to his feet, runs to his foghorn's mouthpiece, and responds to the salute with a rumble that shakes the horizon.

From the lookout, he sees Matvey and Golby, aged ten and twelve, who've made the stretch of beach to the cliffs their own. They score its sand with thousands of neat footprints erased each night, retraced in the morning. The sea destroys everything the boys invent. Osip admires his brothers' resolve, their fight against the intertidal waters. Sometimes they build structures from branches and pebbles and wait to see if they'll resist the waves, sometimes they venture far out onto the rocks, their feet slipping on seaweed, then wait for the tide to come in and watch its advance on the cabin. They don't know how to swim — no one does — but through their inventions and games they ally themselves with the sea all the same. Just as Osip has done with his foghorn.

Sevastian-Benedikt lives in the forest. He spends so much time running through it that he turns into a sturdy giant with green knees and elbows. From the lighthouse, Osip catches the occasional glimpse of him advancing through the foliage. On such days, the eldest returns to feed the clan, carrying on his back carcasses, bags of rice as heavy as dead bodies, the berries he's gathered en route, and the delicacies he's traded for in Seiche. He receives a king's welcome. Thanks to his efforts, the family will eat. He's their provider and the favourite.

Sitjaq empties the day Matvey, Goldby, and their father perish at sea.

One afternoon, their mother complains of hunger — the eldest is taking too long to bring meat and berries. From his lookout, Osip watches his father and brothers: they carry the patched-up boat overhead along the dunes. In their hands are fishing rods, nets, and colourful fish hooks. Osip imagines them whistling the tune of a ribald song as they recede from view and into the woods and reappear farther down. For a while they row erratically, then turn in circles until they find their rhythm and head for the coast beyond the cliffs, out of sight.

They do not return.

For several days, the waves bring in nothing, and then they spit out the youngest brother. Later: blue and yellow planks, a buoy, half a grey oar. Mother Borya buries the relics next to her son; she stares at the lighthouse, the deserted dunes. There's nothing for her in Seiche. Here, there's nothing for anyone.

Sevastian-Benedikt has disappeared into the jungle and has not been back for ten days. Osip holes up in the lighthouse-keeper's office to read whatever he comes across there, especially logs from ships wrecked on the shoals. His mother sits on the porch, her chin resting on her hand, and doesn't move. For a day, a night, another day, another night, until diluvian rains pour down on her, leaking through the roof's blackened thatch and dislodging her.

Four years later, the eldest brother's woman scores the beach with her footprints just as his brothers did before her. The cabin has been deserted for a long time — the Old Woman and her two remaining sons live in the lighthouse now — so the new arrival appropriates it for herself, makes it a part of her territory, which soon extends to the dunes, the forest's edge, the cliffs, the caves.

She has only to shed her dress to disrobe. She has no undergarments to unlace or throw off. She grabs the fabric at her waist and crosses her arms, then in one fluid gesture, hikes the dress over her shoulders, her head, her hair. Stripped of the taffeta, her skin resembles a leopard's — a profusion of round pink and white scars. They're concentrated in the middle of her back, between her shoulder blades, then spaced farther apart; on her ribs and the small of her back they've taken on a rusty brownish hue, as though freckles had sprung up after she was wounded. Other marks streak her buttocks, thighs, and upper arms; on her right calf, faded over time, a thin line stretches from knee to heel and divides her leg into perfect halves.

From the lantern, Osip studies the geography of this stranger. He arms himself with the spyglass and follows the walks she takes along the large lagoons bordering the tower. The woman baffles him. Her wandering makes no sense, she bares her flesh without shame, tumbles in the ocean, dives headfirst, and resurfaces far from shore. She's always on the move, knows how to butcher and hunt, fishes with branches she has sharpened herself, grills her catch over pine-cone fires. She lives on her own in the musty, leaky hut, refuses to use the lighthouse bedroom, remains in the hovel, errant, mute.

Her name is Noé. She is not here to stay. Not that she says as much to Sevastian-Benedikt — he knows.

At the end of September, she expels Mie. The little one glides from between her legs, emits one big cry, then falls silent. The first sound she makes is not even a true wail, more like a breath, a greeting to the world. Mie's face is all eyes, open wide to gorge on the beach and the creatures inhabiting it. All winter, Noé carries Mie on her side like so much baggage. She doesn't speak to her, doesn't fuss over her, but takes her wherever she goes to do whatever she does, beneath her sweaters and dresses, belly to belly, tiny feet striking her hips night and day. Mie learns to suckle on her own, twists to reach her mother's breasts and grips first one, then the other. When she isn't nursing, she sleeps, she chirps; she gazes at the animals and the people, the swirl of the big sea, the stretch of sand along its edge.

The body—it didn't arrive all at once.

At first, the flat nipples turned pink and then protruded, skin pulled every which way—like her other limbs in fact, stretched and elongated until they formed an odd assemblage, arms and legs out of proportion, random curves on her buttocks, on her cheeks and shoulders, on her pubis, swelling quickly as though fat had coiled up inside: this soft new mound, its dense vegetation slowly materializing—one hair to begin with, then ten, thirty—black and thick, quite unlike the tow-coloured hair on her head and the whitish-blond down on her thighs.

And Mie knows it isn't over. Her breasts have turned to fatty buds but resemble neither the exuberant peonies that wilt on the Old Woman's trunk nor the small dahlias planted below Noé's collarbone. She sees herself with a bust somewhere between her grandmother's and her mother's, generous but firm. This is what she imagines without conceiving of the heft and shape of her breasts, or how she'll move differently once her bosom obstructs her torso.

She has always borrowed the bodies of beasts—birds and fish, mammals and tiny insects. She can feel the warm and cold drafts of air under cormorants' wings, water working its way through sharks' gills; her fingers and toes have sensed the contour of stones under foxes' cushioned paws. But when she is not inside another creature's body, she has trouble walking and swims only marginally better. Her feet trip over obstacles, arms stretched wide to either side of her, hands clutching two branches to help her keep her balance. Ten, fifteen times she stops on the path between the sea and the forest and swallows the air in large gulps, out of breath until the sight of a worm, a crab, or a long-billed curlew diverts her. When she buries her mind inside another animal, her breathing returns to normal. Otherwise, her child's body—a young girl's—is a hindrance. It's a body Mie cannot master.

She sits up in bed. The sheet slides down her belly and drops rumpled onto her thighs. She shivers as her back touches the cold stone.

The bedroom is on the third floor of the lighthouse. It's narrower than the rooms below, but when the waves are so high they breach the dike and hammer the tower, water doesn't reach the apertures carved into its walls. The floor is taken up with a wide mattress stuffed with straw, feathers, and sand. Blankets have been thrown across it; at night, her brothers fight over a pink cotton comforter, worn but silky soft. Mie waits for them to start snoring before stepping over the Old Woman, Osip, and little Dé and then, without a sound, trading her bedspread for Abel and Seth's quilt. In the winter Mie wonders if, in the crumbling cabin, Noé has what she needs to keep warm. On such nights she looks for birds flying into shore, but none appear before dawn. Distraught, she falls asleep by the window.

The tower's rooms are taller than they are wide. Above the bedroom, on the highest floor, Osip has set up an office. The logbooks and records for the lighthouse are filed in massive bookshelves built by Sevastian and mounted onto the walls, sheltered from waves and storms. Osip has placed his father's work-table in the centre of the room and displayed all kinds of objects collected by former keepers there: foreign coins, binoculars and telescopes, magnifying glasses, compasses, and an astrolabe only Noé knows how to use. Osip spends his time either in this room, on the gallery, or in the lantern room, lugging his notebooks with him wherever he goes to jot down ships' routes, their country of origin, their size, the temperature, the height of the waves, the tidal tables.

Mie knows that Osip will leave his office to join

her. She listens for his shuffling footsteps on the stairs and, at the sound of rustling, lies back and tries to strike a woman's pose beneath the sheet. She has no idea how to arrange her hair and place her arms if she is to awaken desire. She thinks of Noé. She imagines her mother's outstretched body when at last she falls asleep, exhausted from trekking along the cliffs, from Sevastian and Osip fighting over her, from all the children clamouring for her attention. Mie has never seen Noé relax. Still, she tries to imagine the sleep that overcomes her after dealing with the ardour of the two brothers, each in turn. Gradually, Mie finds the right angle for her hands, torso, and ankles, and then, more or less proud of her pose, she eyes the door.

No one appears.

She is alone with the thought of Osip.

She tries to imagine how it will unfold, the way in which he'll start to caress her, whether he'll hurry or bide his time. Will he pat her cheek and her shoulder first, the way he does with the boys, the way he has done with her until today? She wonders what she would like. If he touches her belly straight off, will she be startled? The idea makes her tremble, whether from excitement or fear she's not sure. Perhaps he'll want to look on her before he tries anything. She pulls the sheet up closer to her chin. Her uncle will be gentle, he knows no other way.

When he covets Noé, he descends from the lighthouse — his feet sink into the sand, he walks like a man who's a stranger to the beach — and reaches the cabin. Mie finds a lizard, a bumblebee, borrows its body and observes Osip, watches him lead her mother over to the bed. All of a sudden, it's as if Noé has become a malleable object; she has no will, she drops onto the mattress, facing the wall, her back to him. He removes her clothing, piece by piece, stares at the fabric of each garment to begin with, then the skin beneath them. He lifts her limbs, one by one, to remove her skirt and her blouse. Noé is without a spine; her arms fall to her sides the minute he releases them, he's the one who lays her body down on the sheet. He frees the bun in her hair. Noé's only movement is to hide her face, which she does without using her hands, turning her forehead so that strands of hair fall across her cheeks, over her eyes. Afterward, she doesn't budge. Osip smells her clothes, her neck; he gathers up her garments, folds them, lays them down on a chair off to the side. Then he looks at Noé: the play of light across her skin, her scars, her shock of hair. Later he joins her, follows the swollen lines along her ribs, caresses her, strokes her head the way Mie pats the kittens, brushes the hair from her face, wanting to see all of her. Still Noé does not budge. She has vacated her body. Osip likes an empty shell.

Once his mind is made up, he undoes his pants without removing them — Mie doesn't know her uncle's naked form the way she does her mother's. He pushes against Noé's white buttocks, grinds his pelvis like the wolves do, not for long — one, two minutes — then stops, sighs, and dozes off, his thick arms wrapped around Noé's breasts, belly, and hips. She remains immobile, almost not breathing, her long dishevelled hair across Osip's face and her own.

Mie sinks into the sagging lighthouse mattress and, to calm herself, repeats over and over that she prefers her uncle to her father, who takes Noé abruptly, hiking up her skirt, pinning her to a wall, a tree, the ground. Sevastian-Benedikt mates like a stag or a drake, without preamble, in one fell swoop, then stands and returns to his forest. Noé stays put, whether on the ground or propped against the cabin; her elbows are scraped, she rubs them with her saliva, rights her dress, detaches wisps of hair from her face, wipes the sand from her cheeks.

Mie wants only to flee from the room so time will pass more quickly. She lies alone, air moving laboriously through her chest — not that she notices — shuts her eyes tight to listen to the sounds inside masked by the din of the waves. She strains to hear any buzzing or chirring announcing the arrival of an insect that might offer her a chance for escape. Silence. As though all creatures have abandoned her.

She lies unmoving, in the position carefully chosen for her limbs.

She rebuilds the tree in her mind. Sevastian-Benedikt is her father, Noé her mother. The Old Woman is Sevastian and Osip's mother, and the younger Abel, Seth, and Dé may be her brothers or simply half a brother each. They have two fathers, which is to say none, as it is impossible to ascertain whether it was Sevastian or Osip who planted the seed for them in Noé's body. All of which means that Osip must have started up with Noé after Sevastian, because otherwise Mie, like her brothers, would be unsure of her father. She is four years older than Abel, the second child, so somewhere between their two births, Osip took up with Noé.

No one speaks of these things, evident to those in the know. It has taken a while for Mie to understand; she has drawn the family tree and its intertwined roots and branches in the sand dozens of times. Often, she has compared it to other trees — the trees of frogs or wolves, cranes, ducks, otters. Nowhere has she found anything similar.

—

She points her toes to make her legs look longer. The angle of one elbow both obscures and reveals her heart, she has slid her other arm beneath her head and pulled her mop of hair behind her.

She's lost in thought. The offspring of other living creatures grow to assume their parents' shape and strength. She has grasped the difference between the sexes. She need only watch Noé and learn the workings of her mother's body to guess at the future of her own. She would like to look like her mother but has inherited nothing from her but her skin — unsightly marks accentuated by the sun; her face, arms, and trunk a mottled collection of brown and white constellations. At twelve, her face is nothing but freckles, thick lips, and pale eyes that stand out against the grime. Her solid frame, her blond hair, her limbs, all like her father's. A snub nose, chalky lips, eyebrows and lashes that turn white in summer; no need for a family tree to know she is Sevastian-Benedikt Borya's daughter in blood and body.

In the bedroom, nothing. She counts the minutes for what seems like ages; she listens for sounds to herald her uncle's arrival.

Osip doesn't appear.

Sun filters through the narrow slits of the windows. The sea is alive with the calls of eider. Several hundred stop at the lighthouse, always on a journey elsewhere. In springtime, to Seiche; in autumn, out to the high seas. When ducklings age, they become like the parent of their gender — the females resemble the mother, the males their father. Mie wishes it were all as straightforward with human beings, but the similarities among humans stop at their hidden organs.

Mie will not grow up to become Noé.

She sighs. Her hand under her skull has gone numb. Her carefully placed fingers curl, her arms fall to her torso, her knees bend, her chin drops.

She dreams she's the beach.

Her body of sand feels everything. By her navel, her little brothers grill rabbit on the embers of driftwood. Her father walks through her forest of hair, sometimes by her ear, sometimes her neck. The lighthouse stands beyond her ankles. At the tips of her toes, Osip keeps watch over the lantern. The Old Woman comes and goes on the path linking Mie's feet to her belly, her son to her grandchildren; she carves the deep footprints of a heavy-set woman along Mie's thighs.

Animals traverse her dunes: lizards, marmots, raccoons, wolves, foxes, deer. Birds swoop by; sometimes she recognizes the draft beneath their large wings. Their landings tickle her but their claws leave no mark on her side. Her slumber continues. She feels the great movements that shape her from below; crabs and worms dislodge the soil and aerate it, tree roots drain the seawater, the surf carries old seeds out to sea and the waves bring in new ones. The dilapidated cabin lies heavy between her breasts. Its moulding timbers nourish the sand. Mie can discern the slow labour of carpenter ants, rodents, and termites breaking up the detritus to build their own nests.

Noé is nowhere to be found. Glass beads, the planking of shipwrecks, and conches as small as fingernails: Mie feels everything, right to the raking of the ocean's waves — but her mother, no. Her mother lives somewhere that is not the lighthouse.

It's the wind that leads Noé to the sea. During a storm, schools of medusas are brought in with the swells and wash onto the shores around the lighthouse. The next day, Noé takes the path down from her cabin, runs her fingers along the dry grasses bordering the trail, steps onto the sand, and digs in her toes. Gusts of wind buffet her; she winds the folds of her skirts around her hands and grabs the jellyfish, one by one or in bunches, collecting them in pails of salt water to be prepared later for grilling on fires of brushwood.

Mie entertains herself by following in her mother's exact footsteps. The Old Woman won't let the little one go barefoot, so Mie tramples Noé's footprints with the hard soles of her shoes. She stretches her legs, leaping to imitate her mother's giant strides before they're erased by the waves. The tide is on the rise and will soon sweep up the brown seaweed again, the crabs and brittle sea urchins, the flotsam and jetsam of shipwrecks. In less than a quarter of an hour, Noé's traces will be swallowed by the surf. Mie runs out of breath, slows down, then drops limply to the ground.

She lies back and hollows out the loose sand with her head, imagines her hair buried in silt. The strands of her hair become roots. From the ends of her hair to her forehead, she taps into the moving soil. She is eleven. Her arms are stretched out in the form of a cross, her palms offered up to the air. She wiggles her fingers, tries to grab the gusts of wind and shape them into cold balls in her hands. Farther on, Noé is bent over a mound of shells, piling up the smaller ones and picking out the larger ones. She sorts through them all, throwing the empty conches back to the sea. When occasionally a shell appeals to her she slides it into her apron pocket. She's singing.

A man killed the goose
To feed his family of four
Later the stag was downed
With arrows that ended their love

Mie wraps herself in song, surf, wind. She tries to sink her being into Sitjaq. Flies walk across her face. Sometimes she wrinkles her nose to chase them off, sometimes she lets them be: their feet are a part of the world she's trying to hear in its entirety.

She's not doing all that well. Dé's cries break her concentration — as do the clacking of shells Noé throws over her shoulder, the foghorn, the call of migrating birds. The tide washes in, foam surrounds her ankles, her calves. The water is teeming with bits of seaweed that stick to her feet. Crabs make the sand by her ears crackle. Too much to absorb: she can no longer discern what to listen to and what to ignore.

You cannot become the earth the way you become a heron, a turtle, a bee.

She opens her eyes.

Seth is above her, his face just a few inches from her own. He is six years old, has thick, bushy eyebrows, Osip's fat chin, Sevastian's forehead, the Old Woman's traits, Noé's hair. He's the only one like that: with his mother's dark mane. Everyone else's is blond, darker or lighter depending on the season. When Mie finally opens an eyelid, he smiles. His child's teeth sit loose between his lips, and he scrunches up his nose, wipes his mouth with his sleeve, spreading a streak of grey dirt from cheek to chin. As soon as he has her attention, he sprints along the beach in jerky gerbil bounds and then disappears behind the rocks.

Mie understands: he's found a creature he wants her to see.

He is six, he doesn't speak, but he loves to be told things.

He leads Mie to the rocky terrain of the northern cove. She doesn't need him to point whatever it is out to her. Before them: a small flock of huge birds, white and grey, necks that are black, part of their wings too, red foreheads. Long legs, slender throats.

"They're cranes."

Seth frowns. He looks at the shore birds, then back at Mie. She says again, "Cranes." He waits. "They aren't dangerous," she adds. Now his expression changes; he turns away, makes a dash for the animals, arms open wide. The cranes draw themselves up to their full height—they're twice as big as he is—ruffle their feathers, and swell their crops, but he's not afraid: Mie said "they aren't dangerous." He gallops till they take flight, the birds panic-stricken by this animal they've failed to impress. Sand rises in a cloud as they spread their wings, Seth laughs and continues his charge, running in circles for a while and then trotting off, his attention drawn elsewhere. He heads for the forest, perhaps to join Abel in his earthen hideout, or to climb a tree and gather honey, Mie doesn't know. She stays standing, watching as he dashes away. Seth disappears between two tree trunks.

She is alone, and perches on a rock.

It takes some time for the cranes to land again. They do so cautiously, survey their surroundings, make sure the rowdy creature has gone. Mie studies them. No chicks, three immature birds, two pairs and a few straggling loners. She chooses a female, smaller than the rest, because she likes her broad forehead and rust-speckled plumage.

She takes a morsel of her being between her fingers. She sighs.

She wishes it were as easy to become Sitjaq as it is to become the crane.

The heartbeats are distinct — low, slow bursts. The pulsing starts in her chest and sets the ligaments of her throat to trembling. Seth's disturbance has accelerated their cadence, but slowly her heart finds its rhythm, her adrenaline subsides, and her body grows calm. Blood no longer needs to be dispatched as quickly to her talons and wings.

Mie is the crane, effortlessly. Her breathing falls into sync with the creature's. Her neck, hands, and legs relax. The bird asks no questions and neither does she. Like the others, she parts eelgrass and flushes out the urchins and mussels hidden underneath. She doesn't taste them. She doesn't smell them. She apprehends their texture with her beak. Rough or smooth. Edible or not. The pickings slide from her mouth to her craw, accumulate against her heart and stay there.

All her attention is focused on her immediate environment: food, predators, the colony. Suddenly, the world is full of simple things — the rustling of grasses at the edge of the forest, the tumbling of shells along the sand, the scrabbling of crabs to be intercepted as they cross the beach. The air is alive with the ardour of spring. Aside from her quarry and the warm breezes, nothing else matters for Mie, though she does feel a quivering, an enticing, a disconcerting warmth that makes her squirm and shift her weight from one foot to the other before she returns half-heartedly to the crabs and rock lobsters. Time passes and the quivering spreads, extending to her wings, which she shakes. It radiates inside her gullet, she puffs out her throat and, finally, unsettled, returns to her meal.

She stretches to her full size, scans her surroundings, and realizes she's not the only one in this state. A male bounds toward her. He leaps high—a metre, if not more. Once he has her attention, he stops, throws his head back, beak open, neck taut. He clatters, lays his feathers flat against his back till they're touching, bows low and straightens, five, six times in a row.

It's all so natural. Mie follows suit. She throws her head back toward her spine, her throat fully stretched: the cry emerges effortlessly, from her belly to the sky. She starts to hop again, her legs weave a dance, she rises just high enough to offer her breast for the male to rub against. Their wings open and close, but they don't take flight. She bows, he stretches, then they both begin to jump. Initially he bounds higher than she does, then she bests him. Theirs is a perfect synchrony of gestures, songs, bodies.

The crane has never experienced anything quite like it. Nor has Mie. When the male mounts her, she hesitates, entertaining for a moment the thought of vacating the animal, but she stays put, she feels the male's weight on her back, she shakes herself, though not to chase him away but to make herself seem bigger. He manages not to nick her with his talons, hangs on to either side of her wings and folds his legs. He's heavy. She lets the coupling take place. It's quick. And appeasing.

When the male pulls away, Mie returns to her own body, her breathing ragged, her limbs rigid on the rock. She touches her belly, her hand on her sweater and then underneath. She strokes the surface of her arms. She caresses the skin along her shoulders where the male planted his long legs. Her palms are cold and her shoulders burning.

The cranes mate before spring has fully arrived. In the northern cove, drifts of snow still melt through the eelgrass. For the longest time, Mie remains with the birds, borrows the crane's body: day after day she lets herself be mounted. Afterward, she caresses her belly, her arms, the hard tips of her breasts; she gives herself over to the gentle touch of her own hands.

When the migration resumes, she looks for other beasts — a wolf, wolverine, vole, mallard, hare, musk-rat, buzzard — all of them rutting or in heat.

Three weeks after the cranes' departure, Sevastian comes upon her sitting on a log where the pebble-bedded river, swollen by spring melt, overflows and floods its banks. Around her, squirrels frolic from one tree to the next. Her father calls out her name. She doesn't respond. She sees neither Sevastian nor other creatures.

She is an otter.

She's held underwater by a male, his jaw clamped tight around her neck.

She struggles, her legs thrashing, her fur sliding against the male's slick body. At times, she surfaces, takes a breath, cries out, whistles; then she's dragged to the bottom again, the other beast has her by the neck, his fat digits around her pelvis. He doesn't let go. Her heart beats, weak but quick. She stalls, he holds on, she fights and fights—lashing out with her whole body, her paws, head, claws, teeth—then all of a sudden, the tension subsides. Water envelops her and muffles all sound. Around them fish are spawning, tadpoles swarming. Air bubbles everywhere brush against her fur. Mie swishes her tail to one side, revealing her nymphae. The male is ready, he thrusts, she lets him, she gasps for air but doesn't fight, the male moves quickly, she lets herself sink. A to and fro carried by the current. The moment of grace lasting less than a minute. Soon she shakes her head, wanting the other otter to release the pressure on the nape of her neck. She's had enough and covers her sex with her tail. He's done his part, their two bodies separate and she resurfaces, swims quickly, climbs onto shore, snorts.

The other follows.

She tries to bite him. He retreats and now she chases him; he runs; he pulls too far ahead, starts to slow down, pretends to flee but always waits for her; at times, he lets her catch up; at others she passes him by and he chases her. They gambol along the riverbank, slide in the mud, run away from and toward each other, clutching and tumbling down the sand to the river, belly against belly, their fur mingling. They lick each other, rub their muzzles, wash their heads, their bodies; cuddle, embrace. Finally, they return to the water, she feels the other's firm jaws around her neck, she thrashes, he takes a firm hold of her pelvis with his paws.

And, later, Mie is a bear. This time, she chooses a male on the prowl. In him, she tracks a female for days — from one nest to the next, one scat to another. Analyzes scents, fights rivals, chases away the offspring of the last litter. She no longer eats. She sniffs. She tracks. Her heavy paws crush dead trunks lying on the ground; June's leaves rustle beneath her steps. Since morning, the she-bear has accepted her advance. Mie can tell by the whiff of her dribbled urine on the pines. She takes her time planning her approach and then, finally, the female stands before her, fat and willing.

Mie plunges her nose into the female's fur, rummages between her thighs. A perfume of rutting. She lifts her enormous paws and lets them fall on the she-bear's back, rubs her head against her haunch, slides her muzzle along her flank from hip to throat and sniffs beneath her chin: a full-body caress. The contact of their coats fills the void of hibernation: the solitary season is promptly forgotten, as is the fasting and the long period of the hunt.

Everywhere, berries have begun to adorn the bushes; mushrooms and roots pierce the soil. Nearby, salmon spawn. Mie is hungry. If she is to service the female, then she must eat. She runs to the eddies, poises herself on the rocks. An icy wave encircles her paws and brushes her belly. The fish wriggle as they swim upriver: Mie catches them in one lunge, her teeth planted in their gut. The salmon writhe in her maw, she carries them to the bank, tears off huge shreds of flesh as they squirm beneath her claws. She crunches down, their tails slap her in the face.

Occasionally, between mouthfuls, she catches the scent of her female. Desire sends a jolt through her body; she flays the fish and gnaws at their flanks. When there is nothing left but bones and a skull, she makes a headlong dash and throws her weight upon the other bear with such force that together the two fall back, mouth to brow, Mie's huge paws on either side of the other's midriff. Then she gets up, buries her muzzle in the she-bear's ribs, nudges her to her feet, moves in behind and mounts her.

She must wrap herself completely around the other's fur and flesh, grapple with the immensity of this beast. The male animal doesn't register the size of the being beneath him, but Mie does. When he thrusts, when he burrows into the she-bear's belly, the young girl marvels at this dive into a warm, living creature. Against the penis, organs palpitate; she can feel the male's heart throbbing in its sex and the she-bear's heartbeats all around her. She bores in, drives, and plunges. Sperm rises and engorges her member, she thinks she will die inside the male — the desire so stupefying it could kill her — but the explosion relaxes the beast's body; Mie returns to herself, to her legs and arms and hands. She touches the ground as though Sitjaq now belongs to her.

Rutting season passes, as do summer's heat and golden light. Mie sleeps in the tower bed. She dreams she is the beach and, during this time, the cold makes its gradual way to the lighthouse. Still, she has covered herself only with the thin sheet reserved for heatwaves. She'd thought its transparency would please her uncle. In her torpor, her thoughts are for him alone—he whom she awaits but who does not come. A creaking of the stairs would surely wake her. The wind blows in from the sea, lifts the gauzy fabric and bares her ankles, her calves. The draft carries the scent of fall and, deep in its gusts, the threat of winter. Mie curls into a tight ball on the mattress, the hair on her legs bristling, her nipples hard, her feet tinged blue. The studied womanly poses are forgotten, her body candid in its young girl's slumber.

A spider drops onto her forehead. Its thread shimmers in the light, its tiny legs tickle her and undo her concentration. She knits her brow, scrunches up her nose, soon moves her head and neck.

In her dream, wave upon wave scrub and ultimately unearth her carcass. She is no longer the beach, she has become herself again. She extricates herself from the ground, brushes off the layers of sand stuck to her arms. On shore, she finds three desiccated eels shrivelling in the weeds and swarmed by insects. Thick skins coated with sticky film, irises burnt by the light, whites like the eyes of the blind, slack jaws showing small, pointy teeth. They are intertwined like lengths of rope, too tangled to be sorted one from the other.

She shivers, both in her dream and in her room. Behind the windows, the sea frays into strands along the coasts. Channels, rivers, and streams wend their way across the continent, divide into deltas, and empty into the estuary northeast of the lighthouse, or into the giant flat ocean stretching to the south and the west.

Wrapped in her thin sheet, Mie continues to doze. She has spent the summer stealing the spirit of cranes and bears. She has learned through them how to mate. But when her father bent her mother over the cabin railing, when Osip rubbed his belly against Noé's inert back, it hadn't occured to her to borrow their eyes, their minds. She hasn't imagined doing with humans what she has done with beasts. And so she lies there, kept from sleep by the significance of this thought: she knows the bodies of animals but nothing of her own.

She squirms.

In her dream, she tries to pick up the eels. At her touch, their corpses turn into cables she absolutely must unravel. The minute she undoes one knot, two more appear. She perseveres, her nails break with the effort, but somehow she must separate the three strands. It has something to do with her mother. At one point, she almost succeeds; instantly, the ropes become three snakes that slither through her fingers, slide down her thighs, and glide out to sea.

She stays onshore and watches them cut across the waves.

There's a rumbling in the air, but the horizon is calm.

III

The eldest brother's woman has short, dirt-encrusted fingernails, but beneath the grime, they are a bright pink. Her fingers are covered in white patches that mottle her tan skin. Slowly, her hands have begun to wrinkle; at the knuckles, they look to be covered in scales, but the skin there is as silky as the skin behind her ears or on the soles of her feet.

This woman's wrist, elbow, and shoulder are linked by two long stalks that trace a path from her nails to her neck. Her hair is matted by the salt of the sea and forms a nest against the nape of her neck. Her back is naked and free beneath her dresses, naked and free beneath the sheet. Her spine is curved like seaweed.

She is asleep.

Osip stands in the doorway to the cabin. He doesn't dare step forward. He doesn't want to leave. He stares at Noé, lying just a few steps away. Her rib cage rising and falling. The damp has turned her skin a lustrous bronze.

Her buttocks not quite covered by the sheet.

Osip stands at the threshold as he did before by the large villa; he breathes in the intoxicating air but doesn't enter.

Ever since Father Borya's death, the cabin has been abandoned. Outside, birch trees are slowly eating away at its walls. The trees are crushing the dilapidated dwelling, vegetation is buckling its planks and windows. The Old Woman and her son live only in the lighthouse now. In four years, this is the first time Osip has set foot on the north side of the beach.

He doesn't cross the threshold. He stares. The room looks nothing like it used to. Overturned bookcases, sunken armchairs inhabited by vermin, curtains torn off and made into rough sheets, books, a fishing rod, a tobacco box, glass beads, shells, dresses, a pipe, an easel, a ladder, an umbrella. Everything in the cabin converges on the bed: the junk, the rust, the light filtered in beams through the windows' filth.

Noé is asleep.

Three posts support the baldaquin. The fourth is broken. The mattress sags in the middle and the box spring has lost a few boards, which haven't been replaced. Netting hangs from the ceiling, gathered up in the middle, dropping in a cascade around the canopy. It's a greyish-beige, ultra-light, something akin to black mould climbing up it. Wind blows in through the door, the windows, the pierced roof; it lifts the netting to reveal Noé's ankles, legs, the supple line of her back.

For ten days in a row, Osip circles the cabin, climbs the mildewed stairs, stands at the edge of the porch but does not cross it. Each time the same: he surveys his surroundings, makes sure the coast is clear, and then approaches; he hides behind the door frame, undoes his trousers, and climaxes quickly, imagining the head of his penis butting up against Noé where the line of her buttocks becomes one with her back.

On the eleventh day, the same again: he watches, ensures there's no one nearby, unbuttons his trousers, but when Noé hears the sound of his hand at work on his penis, she sighs. Then, with a small gesture that means infinitely more to Osip, she pulls back the sheet and exposes herself from chignon to toe.

It takes a long time for Osip to notice her presence. From a distance, he sees nothing but a flaxen mark on the greyish sand of the northern cove. It resembles the shadow of a cloud rolling in from the sea. Osip glances at the boat without noticing it — he's on his lighthouse watch, but his thoughts are elsewhere. He's thinking of Noé's body, the taste of her breasts, the scent of her bush, her thick mane, the contours of her skin that now is half his. The hulls of the passing ships are weathered, like the stranger's back, their flags mirror the colour of her hair, of her lips. Noé is everywhere, except in the dunes of the northern cove.

The boat sits on a stretch of round pebbles that tumble to the coast. It's a small craft made of bundles of bulrushes with a fair-sized hut on top and a birch mast. Osip picks it out when Noé raises the sail. The bluish-grey blemish suddenly appearing on the beach reminds him of the sheet she pulled back a few days ago to reveal her body. For a moment, he thinks of the way she rolled from her belly to face the wall and shivers at the memory of her quivering breast, her weight on the bed. Then his thoughts return to the oddness of whatever this bluish-grey thing is among the northern dunes.

His spyglass is back on the table in the office; he goes down to get it and returns to the gallery. It takes only a couple of seconds for him to adjust the lens and then both stand out clearly against the sand: a boat, and Noé, who has climbed on board.

She's wearing thick canvas pants she must have unearthed among the old rags in the shack. Still heavy with the milk that fed Mie, her breasts are loose under Sevastian-Benedikt's shirt, the wind rushing down her collar and making the sleeves balloon. Colourful bundles lie strewn across the beach, rolls of long paper, small coins, pails, a steamer trunk.

Osip reaches the shore just as Noé has finished storing the rigging beneath the rushes on the deck. She distributes the weight in the hold, attaches the fishing net to the hull. Her cheeks are flushed, her hair braided and away from her face; short leather boots hug her ankles.

This boat is made for travel.

Osip didn't even know she owned a pair of boots.

He advances up the shore. He's carrying ten-month old Mie in a rush basket. Something is making him stagger; he isn't drunk — he doesn't drink—but when he tries to speak, the words clump together in his mouth and come out all garbled. He looks ridiculous. Noé glances neither at him nor at the child he has deposited by the waves. She strips, pulling her blouse over her head with a sweeping motion, the same Osip has seen a hundred times before; there is still flab on her belly from carrying Mie, but to him the loose skin is more beautiful than the once taut flesh, he likes a body that tells a story. Noé sits on a rock, removes her boots, ties them together and throws them onto the boat. She unbuttons her pants; a broad flap covers the front. There are twelve buttons to undo before the pants fall, her breasts quivering each time she undoes another one. She rolls up her clothes and stuffs them into the hut, pushes the skiff into the sea. As she brings her weight to bear on the boat, the shape of the bulrushes is impressed on her flesh. The bottom slides over log rollers, the stones clattering against it sound like maracas. The boat hits the high waves, rocks back and forth, then rights itself and settles on the water.

Other than Noé, Osip has never touched a naked woman.

Mie is whimpering in her basket, she's having trouble breathing; he needs the Old Woman here to soothe the child if he's to find a way to keep her mother from leaving.

The tide is slowly rising. The surf has brought in medusas and Noé makes sure to avoid them as she wades toward her boat. The water has reached her belly by the time Osip's hand seizes her by the shoulder and tugs. A brusque action that makes them both fall back toward the beach, Osip beneath her, Noé covered in brown seaweed that clings to her legs and feet. When Osip tries to speak, the words still bump up against his lips, so he says nothing. Noé gets to her feet, but he holds her back. She's quicker than he is, so he uses his weight to make up for his stumbling. Slowly, the boat drifts toward the reefs. If Noé reaches the open sea, she'll be gone for good. Osip doesn't know how to swim, but she does. She twists and turns in the stones, her skin slippery to his touch, the boat floats away. Suddenly, she has freed herself. One moment, Osip's nose is buried in her hair, and in the next, her feet, ankles, knees, and thighs are submerged. She dives between two breakers and disappears.

Poc.

When Mie hits the water, her body makes the same dull sound as the pigeons falling off the wire in Seiche. *Poc.* Nothing more.

Osip has thrown the baby as far as he is able. The little one floats, then slowly sinks. Noé turns back toward the shore. Osip doesn't move, paralyzed by what he has done. He tries to understand the chain of thought that led him from Noé's hair to the sacrifice of his niece.

Mie is nowhere to be seen.

The boat continues to gently drift.

Osip doesn't know how to swim.

In the time it takes Noé to fish out the baby and bring her back to shore, the boat has capsized, its hull torn from prow to stern by a sharp rock.

Osip returns to the lighthouse, Mie wrapped in his shirt, asleep in the basket. The vessel's cargo floats and scatters along the smooth surface of the water. The ebbing tide leaves behind a few remnants from the skiff and one of Noé's ankle boots. All the rest is dragged out to sea.

Noé gathers up every bundle the tide brings back in. She spreads the bulrushes out on the ground, anchors them with rocks so they don't scatter to the wind, and then, once the rushes are dry, rolls them together and piles them behind the cabin.

After the folly of his act, Osip no longer knows what to do with himself and so he stays in his tower and watches. Noé spends three days salvaging the remains of her boat. On the fourth day, she disappears before dawn and returns after noon, her skin covered in scratches, brushwood under her arm. She sits on the porch steps and sorts through the branches, peels them, then cuts them into sections as long as an adult hand. Later, she digs a hole in the sand beyond the tide's reach. She carries the branches in the folds of her skirt. Its fabric stretches but doesn't tear. She lets the sticks fall into the hole and form a small pyramid that she pats down, sliding her fingers along the wood. She carries stones polished by the sea in the same manner — Osip is surprised at how resistant women's clothing is, delicate but unyielding under wood or stone—and covers the pit with the rocks and then, on top, she piles mud, seaweed and, finally, the dried bulrushes. There in the yellow straw of the boat, the burning begins. Noé makes another dozen trips from the cabin to the fire, feeding the flames with frames and chairs, books, dresses, paddles, canes: her possessions and the Boryas' all in a jumble. Flames leap as high as a lighthouse storey, and the acrid stench of burning wafts far enough into the forest for Sevastian-Benedikt to catch its scent. Inside the cabin, she rips away what's left of the wallpaper, and its glue blackens the smoke as it burns. Finally, she retreats to her quarters and sits on the floor, stares at the empty half of the room, its large wall bare. She breathes.

Osip keeps watch over the fire all night long. He's afraid the flames will spread to the cabin. They don't. Once everything combustible has burned, the flames die; the wind scatters the embers across the beach, leaving the stone mound covered in nothing but cinder and ash.

Osip takes the stairs down from the lantern, trying not to wake Mie and the Old Woman, asleep in each other's arms. Outside the lighthouse, he hesitates. A shallow expanse of water still covers the path linking the tower to the shore. If he waits for low tide and daylight, he won't dare do anything. Only the prospect of a sleeping Noé gives him the audacity to act. He crosses the dunes and imagines her asleep, collapsed from fatigue, half-naked, her dress falling off her shoulder.

He shakes his boots over the first porch step, and sand falls in a cone on the tread.

He pushes on the door into the cabin.

Noé is seated on the floor, she hasn't budged. She's contemplating the wall; at the creak of the door's hinges, she starts, then blinks, as if waking from a dull dream, neither alarming nor pleasurable. For a second, the surprise makes her close in on herself— her chest collapses, her clavicle drops toward her belly, but when she sees Osip, her body grows rigid, her trunk forms a rod, her chin lifts. She stares at him long and hard. Her face betrays nothing, neither anger nor curiosity nor pleasure. She eyes him, and he has no idea that she will never look on him again. Still in the doorway, he bows his head, and when he lifts it, she has already ceased to see him. She concentrates on her wall. The white half of the room seems to devour the whole space. Osip wishes he could fill the silence of the cabin; the void here has pulled Noé to a side of the world where he cannot follow.

Nothing happens for the longest time. He stands on the threshold, Noé focuses on the wall. Occasionally, she squints and tilts her head, as though seeing something she can't quite grasp; she draws curved lines in the dust, then sits up straight and observes in silence once more.

A crow's cawing wakes Osip from his torpor. He steps through the doorway, makes his way to the bed, feet as heavy as lead, and begins to speak. His tongue sticks to the roof of his mouth and he utters whatever comes to mind. "I'll make the bed see I'll just straighten the blankets that's better your pillows don't have enough stuffing I'll talk to Sevastian he can pluck a turtledove you need a comfortable bed I want you to feel at home are you sure you don't want to live in the lighthouse the bedroom is bigger and the mattress soft I could sleep next to you on cold nights the wind won't touch you anymore I want to shelter you here I'll make a fire would you like some tea I always have a few tea leaves with me I'll make you happy let me show you you'll be fine staying here how is it that you have no kindling to start the fire I can use the seat of this chair the leg is broken anyhow."

When Sevastian-Benedikt emerges from his forest, the last embers have died out on the beach. He looks at the lighthouse, which has not burned, and at the cabin gradually buckling within its prison of birch. The fire alerted him, and he's back three days earlier than planned. He pushes open the door. Osip, bare-chested, has pulled Noé's sleeve down, he's leaning over her, studying the burn of an ember that has swollen her shoulder. Sevastian steps into the cabin as if entering his own home, unfazed by the new decor or the presence of his younger brother; though Noé's does surprise him somewhat. He rummages through the objects that have escaped the purge, pulls out a trap with grayed teeth, looks at Osip, "Signs of a bear in the clearing. Tell mother to be careful." Before leaving, he turns one last time and, smiling, looks his brother up and down, "When did you start growing hair there?" he asks. And disappears.

Osip dresses quickly. He does the buttons up on his shirt as best he can, steps out of the cabin, looks for his brother. Three times he circles the house, and then surveys the various trails plunging into the forest, he doesn't even know which leads to the clearing but ventures down one anyway, walking on and on before the thought of the bear slows him down, before the noises begin to worry him, he reasons with himself for half a league then retraces his steps. He'd have nothing to say to his brother in any case.

Noé is on the beach, kneeling before the pyre. She brushes away the cinders that float up and adhere to her face, her arms. Sevastian-Benedikt emerges from the lighthouse — he must have stopped by to greet his mother, his daughter — follows the trail, then lays his trap on the ground; Osip sees him from a distance, would like to join him, but shame holds him back.

Sevastian speaks to his woman, short sentences that his brother can't hear. Osip can't tell if his brother is angry or not. He stays out of sight, half crouching behind the wood piled on the porch. Noé gets to her feet. From his hiding place, Osip wonders if she's looking at his brother or staring right through him at the trees. She lets her dress drop from her shoulders. The top falls to her waist, stops at her hips. Noé pulls the neckline down over her buttocks, in one motion the fabric glides to the sand. Sevastian-Benedikt approaches, grabs her wrist, turns her. With one hand he holds her by the waist, and with the other he forces her to bend. Noé is doubled over his arm. She speaks, the wind carrying her voice to Osip. "Do it," she says. Her legs are two lines perpendicular to the beach, her dress wrapped around her ankles and feet.

For a long while, she stays on the ground as the eldest finishes putting his clothes back on, hikes the trap hanging from its chain over his shoulder, and trudges toward the forest. Osip wishes he could melt into the trees. What could he possibly say? What did Noé give away? He's afraid of his brother's anger, or his mockery, and looks for excuses — she's the one who pulled the sheet away, I was near the cabin, she gave herself to me — but when Sevastian passes next to him, he doesn't even look over; he swerves around his brother and proceeds to the edge of the forest, the trap hanging down his back like the gaping maw of some enormous fish.

He stops only when Osip finds the courage to speak his name.

He's already halfway into the trees by then, the leaves of the trees draw living shadows on his face.

He says, "You can, after me," then turns his back and plunges into the undergrowth; the forest swallows him whole.

The charcoal sticks are wrapped in rags and stored outside the entrance to the cabin. Once Noé had finished scattering the ashes from the bonfire, she dug up the carbonized sticks from beneath the stones, carefully wrapped them in dried seaweed, then the seaweed in cloth and the cloth in a tin box. Fifteen sticks per packet, twenty-two packets in the box and one rag full of broken ends.

Those sticks, it was like she was living off them. Osip watches the ramshackle cabin incessantly, on the lookout for Noé who never steps outside. He trains his spyglass on the porch and counts the disappearing bundles. Sometimes, a hand, a wrist, emerges from the doorway, dips into the box, grabs a bundle, then the door closes and the blond flash of arm disappears.

For two days, he resists. On the third, he comes down from his tower, cuts across the path, climbs the gentle slope to the beach — behind him, waves ferry shells, seaweed, dead fish — and tiptoes up the porch steps. Once at the door, he doesn't know what to do.

At first, he presses his eye to a window pane, but it's dark inside and the window is dirty. He stands and stares at the door jamb for an eternity; finally he gives himself a shake and turns the knob. He tries not to make a sound, but the hinges creak and the door sticks, he has to give it a shove to get it to open. Behind the door, metal pails tip and clatter onto the floor.

Noé doesn't turn around. She's covered in black dust: on her hands, her arms, her face, beneath her nose, her chin, her neck. Wherever beads of perspiration collect, the charcoal adheres, as it does to her blouse and skirt, to the floor, the furniture, and the sheets.

In front of her, the wall is smeared with charcoal. At each end, blank surfaces, grey wood and strips of wallpaper. In the centre, a crude shadowy blotch with moving contours that make no sense. Noé darkens it some more, charcoal floats in a cloud around her hand. In some places she draws the outline of empty patches the size of a fist or a toe. Her gestures are fluid; it's as though she's making it up as she goes. The shadows extend to the blank territory at each end.

Noé lets herself be rocked by the strident screeching of the charcoal on the wall.

She is inside the image, caught up in the long line she continues to draw.

A river born in the northwest that runs to the south of the picture.

Sand on her tongue, in her throat, her nose, her ears, her eyes, in the bend of her elbows, on her knees, her belly, her neck; between her lips and in her opening, too, filled like a conch shell. Sand in her scalp for days on end, that itches and is scratched, sand that falls in fine grains as though her whole skull is nothing but a sandcastle. Crusted hair, a perpetual squeaking in her eardrums, specks disintegrating beneath her teeth, mouthful after mouthful, catching between her molars and gums; sand when she sneezes, in her mucus, in her feces, everywhere. And under the sand's bite, the bite of salt; lesions on her limbs inflamed by the friction of the elements (halite, sediment, water); skin rough for days, months, the healing from huge waves dragging on forever.

Her life began with a drowning, in a meander in the long black line that descends from the top corner of the wall to the centre. Whatever happened in her early years and dragged her into that heavy swell, she does not remember. She came into the world at the age of four tangled in the nets of unknown fishermen, with the sharp taste of rye and the raspy texture of the ocean's bottom on her tongue. Leaning over her: a

huge woman and a man rubbing away layers of mud
with their handkerchiefs. Their faces come back to her
as she traces the river over and over again.

After her convalescence, by order of appearance:

— Wind on salt burns. The cold bite of its
gusts against bared flesh: awakening of the
body within the painful pleasure of senses
heightened by the accident. She scrapes at the
scabs to rip them off, exposes the wounds to
squalls rolling in from the sea.
— The buttery, metallic taste of blood. That
of exposed sores, bug bites, scratches, cleaned
each time with licks of the tongue, even
the tiniest abrasions pinched to release their
claret, her mouth pursed to nurse the wounds.
— The sound of her own voice, explored
in secret in coastal caves. The echo of songs
ricocheting off rock faces.
— Her heels sinking into the silt of low tide.
The slurp of suction beneath her feet, the
ground sticky with seaweed, redolent of salty
kelp.
— The rigidity of her clothes washed in
seawater and dried in the breeze. The cold of
their touch in early spring when ice melts into

the river, the enveloping heat in September when the sun hits their seams and warms the fabric.

— Her shifting shape over the seasons and years, the shooting pain behind her knees as her legs grow, the cloth of her blouse rubbing against the swollen nipples of her budding breasts.

— Slick, muddy rocks and the sharp slice of clams beneath her feet.

Some days, messages from her senses are magnified. Rays of light filtering through the foliage, the sun through slatted fences or the lamp's reflection in newly washed windows trigger strong reactions, sometimes so brutal that she flinches, falls to the ground, her eyes rolling back in her head, and remembers nothing afterward. The fat woman says she's possessed, the man that a physician from the Cité could treat her. Noé doesn't want to be cured, she likes the oblivion that consumes her, the reset to zero of her body and thoughts. For hours before the fits, tension seizes her hands and arms, her legs, heart, lungs: even the air is in excess, takes too much space in her belly. Noé knows that nothing but the black of sheer darkness will soothe her.

Noé's life is on the wall. The expanse of white bordering the river is dazzling. Dust from the charcoal floats above the image, bringing to mind the flocks of ducks and geese that stopped on the shores of the village of Oss on their way north or south.

For fifteen years, Noé observes their flight and envies them. She knows the blue strip of spruce behind the houses and the boundary it forms, and has no idea what lies beyond. The trees look like soldiers aligned in tight rows, they protect the village but lay siege to it, too.

It takes the death of the fat woman and the man for her to plunge into the pine grove and discover the unfamiliar audacity of movement.

Bare trunks topped with cone-filled branches smell of resin, bristle with dry twigs—a labyrinth for insects and birds, especially woodpeckers, nesting in the boughs, also June bugs, and termites that tunnel their holes between tree bark and sapwood. On the ground, a carpet of yellow needles that creatures cross, leaving no trace. A damp circle, the vestige of late summer rains; a warmth different from that in the village, this one less breezy, and sheltered from the open sea's moods.

Noé doesn't draw the woods. She only traces water-ways, though in the blank space to the north of the drawing she's aware of the pine grove that can be crossed in less than an hour — a fake dense forest to keep the village children to the same hard life as their parents. Beyond, prairies stretching as far as the eye can see.

Over and over, she sketches the river's dark lines, opens them to the sea. Her palm travels along the coast, she digs estuaries, rivers, lakes, follows the waterways, finds her homes again.

The filthy tents of a circus; a forest of blue huts; the partly submerged cloister of the Sisters of Sainte-Sainte-Anne; an oilcloth stretched between two trees, every night under different leafy boughs, across thirteen hundred square rods of green, golden, russet, and white fields; northern peoples' shelters on the ice-covered taiga; old tubs and actual ships that toss, pitch, and rock; the baggage compartment of one train, another's boxcar; mountain isbas; the deserted castle at Luce-aux-Farolles; coppices of birch and cedar, rabbit warrens, beech, almond, and fig groves; thatched farés; gîtes and hovels; Father Libouban's hermitage; gourbis with walls of sand; caves; countless stables, cottages, and chartreuses; harbour warehouses and noisy factory hangars; church squares, temples; the gaudy windows of greasy smelling restaurants, the cots of Ismador's boarding school, the attic of the Cité's Opera house, then its grand train station.

She shades in the Bastindale River; above, she imagines flamboyant fields of wild mustard, and coastal villages identical to one another with their clotheslines and painted cottages: Lastaigne, Sérodes, Marydales, Bounia, Nan Mei. She reaches the open sea—the squeak of charcoal resembles that of ice ferried by the tides—and moves on to the ochre earth of the pigment quarries of Oronge; once more she hears the chant of the Circé grottos, the echo of waves against rock walls; and then, when the black mass of water swells into a bay, an ocean, she discovers again the first of the washed-up medusas announcing the welcoming beaches of Sikkim and Saint-Samovar; and finally, the cliffs of Triglav, the remote village of Seiche. Sevastian's forest.

Sitjaq, she has drowned in the sea. It's not on the map, it's not on the wall, she has smudged its spit of sand, its rocks and lagoons, until they merge with the waves and leave no trace.

Osip is standing behind her. For a good while, he studies the drawing, understanding nothing. He backs up. He steps over the objects piled on the other side of the room, leans back against the partition wall, and examines her work from a distance. The blotch, Noé's broad gestures. The drawing tapers off at both ends. Osip looks for meaning; doesn't see black as water, white as land. He thinks he's looking at the scribbling of a madwoman.

The charcoal crumbles, squeaks, Osip loathes the grating sound. He walks across the cabin, draws near, gently takes Noé's hand, distances her from the wall. He doesn't put his arms around her but leads her like a living bird, from the sea to the bed. One by one, he separates her fingers, the charcoal makes a gleeful sound as it strikes the floor.

The ocean is opaque, dotted with small dusty islands in the shape of ripe fruits. Noé has seen them on maps, globes, she has drawn them a hundred times: the curves and hollows and jagged edges of the coastlines, shoals, coves. She loves their contours, the movement of her hand following the shore. The geography of the Dark—this sea with its scattered atolls and sand islands—adheres to her own. Her sketches disappeared with the sinking of *La Coquille*, swallowed up by the ocean along with her rush bundles, but she has not forgotten them.

Drawing these wild lands, the islets lost in the waves, she feels again beneath her feet the texture of soils on which she has trod — silt, gravel, pebbles, sand, the soft humus of old forests, logs, stones, cobblestones; in the cabin, she lets herself be led by Osip, but beneath her toes she can feel the fifteen years of her peregrinations climbing her ankles, her calves, her legs.

Osip steers her across the room. She is nothing but a body. Her limbs sway like buffeted reeds; her heels drag along the floor, no one left to bid them to lift up. Her buttocks are the first to sink into the mattress, then her back, her shoulders, her head; it's Osip who initiates her movements, directs them, chooses them.

Morning's gusts beneath her dress, on her bare thighs and hips as she washes her buttocks, her hands, her face in rivers and ponds.

Her limbs' exhaustion after days' worth of walking and portaging.

The trickle of warm water, from her lips on the leather drinking pouch to her belly, when night falls and snowmelt sputters on the brush-fed fire. At the same time, crickets, frogs, cicadas; evening's echoes replace those of the day. That hour of calm when sounds cohabit.

Noé doesn't shut her eyes. To do so would mean she'd have to order them to close—lower her eyelids, join them together—but she is neither present nor able. Her lashes remain half-open, her mouth too, soft, round; the simple pressure of the shaft is enough to cause her lips to part even more.

The ocean and prairies, shimmering alike when traversed by the wind.
The body's travel through landscapes.

Osip climaxes quickly, his sigh brief. Noé lies still, a tangle of hair and blackened clothing. For a moment, he looks at her, doesn't know what to do. Then, calmly, he rearranges the furniture, the trunks, and the jumble cluttering up the congested half of the room. Against the drawing's dark form, he places a table and three chairs; he finds a cracked vase, he washes it and centres it on a cloth. He steps out, gathers chicory and asters, and sets the mauve bouquet in the middle of the table. When he finally leaves, he has trampled whatever is left of the charcoal sticks and swept their dust between the floorboards. He has made tea.

Noé stays on the bed, a dirty thing in a tidy house. She doesn't move. She has gone.

IV

When Mie draws the otters' tree, its branches head off in every direction, intersecting often, but always broadening toward the sky; they sprout shoots again and again as buds are born and procreate in turn. The bears' tree has heavy boughs that have time to thicken before new scions grow. On occasion, shoots meet, form a knot, and separate farther up. Its branches grow slowly, give little fruit, but its roots are deep and its bark hard.

Mie sighs. By comparison, her tree is a ridiculous sapling. The Old Woman as the skinny trunk, then Osip's and Sevastian's branches intersecting so often it's hard to distinguish between them and finally Noé's furtive stalk grafted to the bole, rootless, without origins. Life has pruned the other shoots: as for this tree, all that remains is the hope represented by four twigs — Mie and her brothers — but there is no one around to be grafted there.

Mie is alone in the lighthouse bedroom. She's wearing her grey skirt and woolen underpants, the worn camisole, the blouse, the cardigan with its wooden clasps knitted into the fabric to keep it from falling apart. She has not yet undressed for Osip. He said "after the noon ships," which isn't now but another two hours away. As she waits, her clothes keep her warm. Mie doesn't want to discard them yet; she wouldn't know what to do with her nakedness. She sits on the foot of the mattress, her knees pulled up to her chin, her arms two dead weights hanging by her sides, hands barely showing at the ends of her sleeves.

She sketches in the dust. She can trace the Borya tree with just one hand, clenching her fingers at first and then opening them as they climb to the crown. She keeps coming back to the branches, trying to find a way to have her own intersect with her uncle's without making the picture meaningless.

It's impossible.

She goes over the lines again and again, dust forms small mounds on either side, and the deformed tree looks like an oversized shoot climbing to the sky in a straight line. There are no ascendants, no descendants left, nothing but a weaving of threads that have become infinitely entangled. Mie loses her temper, erases the drawing with the sole of her foot. Clumps of sand and pollen stick to her sock, she falls back on the bed in the shape of a star.

—

The walls are clad in soapstone tiles, some of them carved by Sevastian-Benedikt and others here before him. Theirs are ragged shapes wrested from the sea — whales, narwhals, crabs, sharks, squid, sirens, seahorses — to which Sevastian has added his forest of bears and wolves, of course, also wild geese, frogs, herons, field mice, ferrets, and owls watching over the children when night falls and one father is at the lantern, the other in the woods, and the mother in her wild woman's lair. It's a room full of silent chaperones that keep watch but say nothing.

The large ceiling tiles are untouched. Mie, stretched out on the bed, observes the checkered pattern made by their connecting joints. For years, she'd fall asleep by assigning a square to each person in her family. Closing her eyes, she'd try to imagine how to people the spaces, filling them up with precious objects belonging to her little brothers, her uncle, her father, the Old Woman, to Noé.

For what seemed like forever, the ceiling and the beach were her only blank pages. Outside, she outlined in the sand huge grid patterns in which she'd pile up rocks, feathers, shells. Here was Osip's house, there Sevastian's, and finally Noé's sprawling territory with, at its centre, Mie's square. For her tenth birthday, Sevastian gave her a notebook and chalk pastels he'd bought in Seiche. She worked in it for eighteen months, and when there was no room left, she traced over the initial images: layers and layers of notes on the same creased paper.

Mie straightens up. As she waits for the appointed hour when Osip will come down to her, she decides to leaf through her notebook. It's hidden under the mattress by the wall. To retrieve it, she has to lift a corner of the bed; the straw mattress is heavy, so she heaves it up with both hands and uses her foot to drag the book out. She catches her breath, then wraps herself in the soft duvet, settles in by the window, unbundles the book from the cloth.

She doesn't know how to read words.

Hers is a quest undertaken by means of pictures and invented symbols. A vertical line for the Old Woman (|), the same line followed by a dot for Sevastian (|·) and two for Osip (|:); an empty circle for Noé (O) cleaved with one vertical Borya slash for Abel, two for Seth, and three for Dé. And lastly, a coloured-in circle that represents her (●).

Her mark for Noé takes up virtually all of the cover. As soon as she was given the notebook, Mie dipped her finger in ink and traced the big circle. The rest of the cover she left blank. *Noé.* She had no desire to add anything more. She'd inscribed the O as if it were the title of her quest and kept the rest for inside.

She opens the book, skims the notes, studies the

diagrams and images, the scribbled-on paper. Patterns repeat, accompanied by drawings of animals that resemble nothing at all, though Mie recognizes them: a rabbit, a stingray, a dog, a grasshopper, a wolf, a crow. Between the various scrawls, she has drawn line after line of detail: the particular habits of each, their way of moving, eating, of being with others.

Mie reads her hieroglyphics in clusters, like sentences.

— Noé burns what she no longer wants to see.
— The Old Woman tilts her head from side
to side as she walks, forehead leaning over her
toes. She never looks up from her feet.
— Abel kneads his sex in the palm of his
hand. He continually squeezes and releases it.
— Noé lives off grilled jellyfish and raw seal,
apples gathered on the cliff, blue rice and
clams.
— Sevastian kills rabbits by breaking their
necks over his knee.
— Seth cries whenever Sevastian kills a rabbit.
— Abel's fingernails smell like chives and
rancid butter.
— Osip's eyes are as big as his spyglass.
— Noé has skin you want to live inside, a
neck, belly, arms, hands, and buttocks to

settle on. Everyone wants the warm space
between her thighs, everyone wants her cheek,
her mouth, her armpit.

On one page, Mie has drawn O and a white doe
being chased by dogs. With her forehead pressed
against the window, she gently rubs the image. Chalk
crumbles and stains her finger.

By day I'm a girl, by night a white doe.
Dogs from the castle all night are my foes.

Noé's songs never reach the bedroom. The din of
waves crashing against the reefs swallows up voices
and the sounds of the beach. The Boryas don't speak
much in the lighthouse because it would mean shouting all the time.
Mie extends her legs, stretches, unfolds. She's sitting in the rocking chair, its large rockers shaping the
sand strewn across the floor. The day she drew the doe
in her notebook was the day her mother sang the song.

Three times over the brass trumpet sounds.
The third time it blows, the doe is brought
    down.

Noé was busy gathering pine cones by the cabin,

then plunging them into the jars of alcohol she piled up by the kindling and logs. (In winter, when she lights the fire, the Old Woman removes a pine cone from a jar and places it in with the branches. Flames mount and the scent of resin fills the air.) All the while, Noé was softly singing the scary ballad to herself, half the words in her head only, the other half crossing her lips. Mie sat crouched beside her, scribbling down a sequence of symbols meaning, "Noé's wrist strains when she breaks twigs."

Let's summon the butcher to skin the creature.
Who said when he saw her, "There are no
    words…
This doe's hair is blond, her breast but a girl's."
Then he pulled out his knife and he quartered
    her.

Sevastian-Benedikt tramped home from his forest, setting the earth to rumbling under his big boots. Noé raised her head, craned her neck, pricked up her ears, listened for a moment to the crunch of feet on leaves, then bolted through the trees without a sound. Mie was still crouched by the half-full jars when her father spotted her and, with a frown, said only, "Your mother?" Mie shrugged, returned to her notebook, and drew in the animal's brow with white chalk.

Sevastian plunged back into the forest, tracking Noé as the dogs did the doe.

Go ahead and eat, I'm the first to take a seat.
My head in the dish, my heart in my feet,
It's my blood that through the scullery seeps
On your grill of black coal my poor bones
    and meat.

Wrapped in her duvet, Mie stares at the animal's muzzle, at the white tufts of hair and the grey mass of dogs — a whirlwind in pursuit. Then she turns the page. On the next, O is linked to a beast no longer a doe. A swan, a buzzard, a salamander, a she-wolf, a siren. Her mother's face as changing as the seasons. What she knows: her father is a lynx, her grand-mother a fox, Osip an owl, Abel a hare, Seth a dog. Dé is too little, but already she'd swear he's a lizard. Her mother? She doesn't know. She wishes she could catalogue Noé in her bestiary the way she has done for the others, but her mother escapes her. Mie goes through her notes, cross-references, compares them. She is forever looking for Noé, who is everywhere and nowhere at once.

— Noé's lips are dark and often closed.

— Noé sings.

— Noé doesn't speak.

— When she does, her voice pulses softly,
then grows in intensity as words cross her lips
and collide with the forest, the rocks, and the
waves of the sea.

For instance, it happens that a sperm whale beaches and dies without water. It lies there for hours and nothing transpires; at the end of the day, Noé leaves her cabin, her arms laden with blades and pails, hooks and sticks. The children have lost interest in the cachalot. To begin with, they climbed it, touched it, their clothes in need of a wash now, given the cadaver smell. Abel wanted to scrape the inside of its eye to know its texture; with Seth, he propped the huge mouth open with a stick and they slipped inside, grabbed its teeth and shouted down its throat, hoping to hear their echo return from its belly. Afterward, they returned to their hideout.

Noé never speaks unless she feels the need. Sometimes, words push against her lips and so she utters them; they are addressed to no one, or perhaps to herself, but not even that is certain. Mie sticks close by, always, not wanting to miss out on those moments.

On the day her mother prepares to skin the whale, Mie plunges her being into the head of a crab — her little crab legs barely touch the ground when she scuttles — but she can still make out Noé's clear, low voice and her characteristic accent, "The ogre in his castle loved the Queen of Saba." Immediately, Mie leaves the creature to its sand nests, her departure so quick that she staggers for a moment and swings her arms in circles to keep from falling. She regains her balance, then approaches her mother, sits by the fire. Noé is bent over a knife as long as a child's thigh. She scrapes the metal against rough rocks, then cleans it, moistens it, whets it again; she pinches the blade between her thumb and index finger, measures its sharpness. When she decides it's sharp enough, she attaches it to a shaft, wraps the handle with strips of cotton, pulls the fabric tight, and tests the sturdiness of her spear. She has no thought for the daughter she doesn't even see, absorbed as she is by the smells of carcass and iron.

The ogre in his castle loved the Queen of Saba.
And though each night, young girls he'd eat,
He'd never lay a finger on the kingdom's queen.

Mie's young siblings come running. Whenever she listens to Noé, their sister's posture changes. She's less guarded, her shoulders broaden, her head sits taller on her neck. They can read her stance from afar, her

straight back announcing a story. They move in—
Noé's voice carries, they don't need to sit too close, and
though they want to hear, they also want to be able to
run away because often their mother's stories frighten
them. They separate, each sitting in a spot of their
own, Seth as far as possible from the cadaver, Abel
half-hidden in a thicket between the beach and the
woods. The sounds they make help Mie locate them,
but she doesn't turn around: she's busy observing her
mother. Noé has raised the spear above her head and,
with one great thrust, sinks it into the beast's hide.

Silently the Queen watches as he
Seduces damsels; the pretty ones you see
"Look then on my treasure chests!
Brocades, furs, sumptuous fabrics,
Moonstones, diamonds, rubies shining,
The crown with every sapphire glowing!
My fortune, my gold, should you give
    yourself to me,
Will henceforth adorn your body and your
    sheets!"

Soon Osip is there, he who never ventures onto the
beach; as soon as the triangle of children has formed
around Noé, he appears; he comes down from his
tower and approaches, always standing too close, his

fat man's shadow swallowing hers. Today, the beast
sickens him, the stench of raw flesh, the bubbling
blood. He stays behind Seth, torn between the lighthouse and Noé.

But to the Queen he never spoke thus
For she had no need of any king's riches.
Only maps and globes, Far Eastern parchments,
It was for the maps and only those maps
That one grey autumn day, the Queen of Saba
Ventured out and set foot in the ogre's castle.

Before she starts skinning, Noé has extracted the
teeth of the whale. They have the shape of an adult's
fingers, are thicker than thumbs; she throws them
haphazardly into a cardboard box. Blood from the
gums has crusted on the ivory. The Old Woman,
without saying a word, has brought out a cooking
pot, a brush, and soap. She sits on a rock by the fire
and begins to clean them. One by one, she polishes
them until their yellow-white is smooth, then lays
them out on large cloths to dry. She rocks Dé in his
basket, smiles; she even suffers through Noé's stories
without her customary sighs. The Old Woman knows
how much ivory is worth; soon she will send her son
to sell the teeth to Seiche's merchants.

As for Noé, she holds her spear in both hands,

gouges the ridge from the tail to the head, the thick skin, the blubber and, underneath, the cachalot's flesh. She chants the story, her voice following the movement of her hands: when the blade thrusts, she recites a verse, when the blade retreats, she breathes in, readies herself for the next.

The Queen lived naked, the ogre oft caressed
Her necklaces, boots, earrings, and bracelets.
But never on that gold-sequined skin had he
    dwelt,
Nor on her figure nor hair: her body too sacred.
He told her, "I love you," and behind him left
His young wife in white and her entire cortège.

Noé finishes the first cut and lays down her spear. Blood has sprayed and spattered everywhere — at her feet, on her skirts, on her hands, her face — and runs in rivulets to the sea. The waves turn crimson, the white sand turns black. The stench of decaying carcass, iodine, and iron catches in throats. Mie shudders. She doesn't understand everything her mother says, doesn't know what an "ogre" is, what "sequined," or "brocades" means, Noé's stories are full of strange words that speak of neither animals nor the sea.

But the Queen of Saba continued to ignore
His supplications, overtures, the way he fawned
    ever more;
And left in her train, by returning to her globes
The ogre, his newlywed, and their sinister ban-
    quet orb.

  Noé stokes the fire. The flames surge in a gold dust high above the beach, sparks take flight and land: on her clothes, where they burn a hole then vanish, on the whale's carcass, in the Old Woman's hair, even on the children's arms whenever the wind turns in their direction. The smoke masks the stench of blood, its white column stands out against the red of the sky.

Noé pauses for a moment, stops speaking, watches the glowing embers, nothing more. No one moves, all that remains is the sound of lapping waves and the brush polishing ivory; the little ones imagine a palace like the lighthouse only bigger, with sails stretched over the windows instead of dirty, threadbare sheets. Chairs with matching legs, pillows full of stuffing, and dozens of pink duvets.

Then Noé picks up the blade again, follows the same route from tail to head, cuts into the left flank, eight metres of skin to carve off, the spear slicing through the hide as though it were butter.

They ate pheasant, mutton, venison,
On wine and mead they soon were drunk,
Devoured profiteroles, flans, then candies,
Turkish delight and August's strawberries.

Enclosed in the thicket, Abel's jaw drops. He once tasted a caramel Sevastian brought back from Seiche and relives the sweet taste of sugar on his tongue, dreams of platters of candy just like that caramel, tempting in their wax wrappers; now he understands the ogre's good fortune: there is no one richer than a man able to eat all the sweets he desires.

At last, he undressed her and looked long
        and hard
On her skin, her white thighs, her belly,
        her breasts,
Then he sliced her in two and cupped in
        his hand
Her bloody intestines and her still-beating
        heart.

Almost imperceptibly, Seth shifts closer to Osip. Mie hears the sound of his bottom sliding across the sand and his quick, scared child's breath. Night falls and Noé's expression is frightening with its dancing shadows, blood, and blaze of light: Seth mustn't cry, says Mie to herself over and over, "Seth mustn't cry." Her brother curls into a ball, bites down on his knee, but holds his sobs inside.

Day after day, for what seemed like forever,
Desperate for love, unhappy, and violent,
The ogre married at dawn and killed
    come sunset.

Soon, all kinds of scavengers draw near to the carcass. Mie worries when crows from the woods begin circling overhead. They caw in the dark and gather in greater and greater numbers, and her first thought is "the wolves will be next." She imagines being devoured by the pack, their fangs boring into her the same way Noé's spear dug into the whale. Her blood mingles with the cachalot's; her mother turns into a she-wolf, eats her child. Mie feels sick, she's dizzy, she has to clutch at the sand to stop herself from toppling over.

The day arrived when the Queen did quit
Consulting her maps and books and globes.
Then announced her departure forthwith.

Noé has finished the second cut, lays down her spear, finds a hatchet and grabs hold of it with both hands; she strikes the tail again and again, blood spattering — a fine rain — and she continues until the last vertebra gives way and the flukes fall to the ground. Then she wipes her face with the back of her sleeve, rubs her eyes with her arms; all she manages is to smear blood over her skin and the fabric, now saturated with blood like everything else.

The ogre, driven mad, threw himself at
   her feet,
He clutched at her legs and embraced
   her knees,
Promised her travel, jewels, the earth and
   the sea.

For the hide to be secured it must be separated from the blubber. Noé lodges a large hook in the severed flank where, barely five minutes before, the tail hung limply. She hoists herself up on the carcass then, using her body as a counterweight, tugs on the skin that separates into a single unbroken pink strip. Once she reaches the end, she uses her blade to detach the epidermis — a tissue eight metres long and two metres wide — from the blubber. In a few days, she'll scrub it in the sea to remove the residue, attach it to a wood underlay, remove all the flesh, melt the whale's brain in water, tan its hide, wait another week, then beat it,

smoke it, and ultimately nail it to the cabin floor to
keep the cold and the winter at bay. With whatever's
left over, the Old Woman will make shoes, bags, belts.

The beauty refused both a halter and a
    wedding,
While the ogre blocked each exit, made a cage
    of his dwelling.
He bolted the Queen in a high, white tower,
Visited every day, tried his luck by the hour.

For the time being, it's the fat that interests Noé:
she carves it into chunks piled away from the fire,
then sets a large cauldron on the flames and liquefies
the blubber inside.
The air smells of smoke and melted cachalot.
Around the blazing flames, it's the blackest of nights.
The children are frightened and hungry, too.

At last, one fine July morning, the Queen
Did greet him and bid, "Have a seat."
She caressed his shoulders, his belly, his
    maypole;
Her breasts swung loose, her thighs bare
    and blond;
She kissed the ogre who could hold it
    no more.

Blissful, ecstatic, and sated with delight
He fell asleep beside her and started to snore
Then woke like a goose to a skewer through
	his side.

Mie breathes quickly, breathes loudly. Osip takes
a step back. Abel quakes in the bushes, their leaves
have been rustling and shaking for some time. Seth's
teeth are still embedded in his knee, he rivets his gaze
on the blood that dirties the waves, can't stop watching it trickle. Dé sleeps in his woven basket. The Old
Woman, her polishing of ivory finished a while ago,
scowls as Noé stirs the blubber in the pot, then empties it into tin pans and leaves their contents to harden
far from the tide's edge.

Around them, crows, rats, foxes, and flies
have started to feast on the exposed flesh; they've
approached without a sound, the fire keeps them far
from the children.

Noé melts the last chunk of lard. She doesn't speak
for what seems like an eternity. She stares at the waves
reflecting the flames and shimmering gold; blood
stains her face, her arms, her clothes.

I know all this for I was there too.
I saw the treasure, the furs, the girls sliced
	in two,

The ogre's huge mouth, his belly full of brew.
When back to front he felt the thrust of
   a dagger
The silver blade was mine, a weapon forged
   in Saba.

Without warning, she bends over, scoops up a pot of wet sand and throws it onto the embers. The entire beach fades to black. Seth sobs so hard, the crows flap their wings and caw.

—At times Noé looks you in the eye and you'd think she is blind.

—Noé hears when you speak to her.

—Noé doesn't respond.

One time Mie asks, "Who told you those stories?" and Noé says nothing, but a few seconds later, she rubs her neck and flings back her loose hair.

Mie knows her mother's gestures by heart. The way she draws shapes on walls, paper, rock faces, and in the sand, always the same. The bend to her wrist as she snaps off a reed. The spontaneous stretching of her neck, the curve of her lower back when the wind picks up and swells beneath her skirts. The way she eludes Dé when he comes up to her, reaching out his chubby hands.

This gesture—the one where she stretches her arms behind her head and pulls her hair away from her scalp—is nothing unusual in itself, but in the register of her mother's movements, this one is new and Mie is struck by it.

From then on, Mie tries a new sentence every day. She says, "I met a blue lobster in the lagoon." "The oldest wolves lead the pack." "Have you ever seen a giant octopus?" She scrutinizes her mother, her goal not necessarily to elicit an answer but to measure the impact of her words by the expression on her mother's face. Noé may not speak, but her forehead, eyebrows, and eyes reveal silent things.

— I like the sound of the bells on your arms.
— What is the language of the country where ships come from?
— Osip calls out to you when he sleeps.
— Why do you have scars on your back?

Sometimes, Noé's belly contracts, or her hands tremble, and Mie knows her mother has heard her, knows Noé isn't deaf as the Old Woman claims. When she chooses the right sentences, Mie draws her mother in.

— Cargo ships are like floating cabins.
— I wish you'd say where you come from.
— Why is this place called Sitjaq?
— Do you believe in omens?

For hours at a time, Mie tends to her words. She tests out their sounds on the lagoon, listens to the echo of their syllables on cave walls. Then, when the sun drops into the sea, when Noé is sitting on the planks of the porch, she plants herself in front of her mother and delivers her sentence.

— Seth has three moles on his left ear.
— I've realized that you like short names best.
— Pelicans walk on water before taking off.

Each occasion is a confrontation. Mie inhales deeply, must let enough air into her lungs for every word to be audible.

— Salt changes the colour of flowers.
— Do women always have two men each?
— Dé eats everything he finds on the ground.

Her mother's gaze grazes her but doesn't linger; it passes right through her daughter's stomach and torso and dirty hands so Noé is staring at the ocean.

— Why do you stay here?

On this day, her stubbornness is rewarded.
"Yes. Once I saw a giant octopus."

There are times when Noé still sings "Let's eat the whale, gnaw on the flank of the water that swallows us up," or the other fable about the ailing wolf and fat mastiff, to the point that Mie, leafing through the pages of her notebook, no longer knows if her mother is the white doe or the skinny wolf or even the whale "whose skin and blubber we separated."

Noé isn't the dog.

Mie shuts her notebook. She lays her face against the cold stone of the lighthouse. The windows of the bedroom are oblong slits, tall enough for the light to filter in, narrow enough to keep the rain out during storms. She leans her forehead on the window frame. Her face is too broad to fit through the opening, but her nose and eyes are exposed to the cool air, her cheeks are mashed against its sides. She wishes Noé would appear on the beach but sees nothing other than her brothers play-fighting with branches.

A great heron is on the cornice, drying its feathers. It stands tall, its neck proffered to the wind's gusts, its wings outstretched and tilted toward its legs. It is so close that Mie could reach out and touch it. She says "Hello," and it turns its head, jabs its beak at her. She stretches too, presses harder against the casing of the window, her throat free, her forehead crushed against the stonework. The bird and the girl observe each other, the wind whips them both. Then the creature returns to its sunbathing and Mie's face withdraws. She takes a few steps back into the centre of the room. The five windows open onto the beach, the cliffs, and the ocean. Offshore, the freighters look like red bricks bobbing on the waves.

Mie's heart skips a beat.

Osip said, "After the noon ships."

The ships have appeared.

In winter, the white of snow and sand become one. A degradation of grey between earth and water. A dormancy that lasts three months. The cold gnaws at everything: the beach, the forest, the rivers, the sea, the cabin, and the lighthouse. Cargo ships pass the lantern and enter the estuary only to be blocked by ice, some for a few hours, others for a number of days. Osip watches for the men to abandon ship, jump onto ice floes, and try to reach shore. Sometimes one will drown; the others make their way to Seiche and wait for the ice to break up and melt into the sea, after which they return to their vessels, repair scraped hulls, continue on their journey. For several weeks, three or four dozen ships sit immobile at the mouth of the great river, patiently waiting.

When he feels the storm brewing, Sevastian comes in from the forest. Osip doesn't know if he does so to shelter himself or to watch over his brood. The eldest brother nails boards over windows, blocks openings in the lighthouse. The wind whistles and strikes the wood. In the bedroom, all is dark. Waves break over the rocks, carrying ice and driftwood.

Noé stays on her own at the other end of the path. The windows of her cabin quake. She often goes out, wrapped in furs pilfered from Sevastian's catches, wears men's shoes found somewhere in the tumbledown cabin, the footprints she digs in the snow twice as broad as her own feet. Gusts lift her hair, cold bites her face. She keeps her forehead high, a woolen sweater wrapped around her head: a splendid queen in the whiteness of winter, crowned with the crimson wool and draped in the pelts of deer, wolves, foxes.

Osip's attention shifts back and forth between her and the ships. The horrific cold on the gallery often forces him inside. He retreats to his office, blowing into his hands. Every hour, he steps outside again. He scans the stationary ships, monitors the shore. He makes sure Noé hasn't frozen, stuck somewhere in Sitjaq's snow. He watches for her. There she is, bent over blue pack ice deposited by the waves, nailing hides over the cabin's windows, stoking a fire as tall as a man, eviscerating a seal.

That first month, the tower reverberates with Abel's cries and Seth's energy. The boys climb to the top of the lighthouse, drop pebbles collected over the summer down the inner staircase. Some rebound, some shatter, others tumble all the way to the cellar and come to an abrupt halt once they hit the wall at the very bottom. Wrapped in blankets and woolens, and warm under the jackets her younger brothers shed in the course of their trips up and down, Mie acts as referee. She crouches in the cellar, leaning back against the algae eating away at the seams of the lighthouse, listening for the clattering of stones down the stairs. Sometimes the sounds match, sometimes the clamour of one stone's fall makes its surpassing of the other obvious. The boys hold their breath — Osip, seated at his desk, is grateful for the silence that accompanies the headlong descent — and sometimes, right at the last second, the pebble in the lead explodes as it hits the edge of a step and rolls to a standstill in a corner by the wall. Then it's the runner-up that triumphs and Abel's cries give Osip a start; he knows by the tone of the boy's voice who has won, who has lost. He takes a long swig of tea, closes his eyes. Soon Abel and Seth have climbed back up the five floors to go at it again — and again, and again. All day long, Mie keeps track. In the evening, the winner of the most races gets the pink quilt and the warm spot in the middle of the mattress.

The boys' whole technique is focused on choosing the right racing stones. In summer, Osip sees them proceeding at low tide far into the dunes, where pebbles have been burnished by the sea's relentless to and fro. They choose them as spherical as possible, prefer-ably heavier, smaller ones, everything a question of the right mix of size and weight, the ore's resistance, the uniformity of its roundness. In the fall, they polish them, clean off any residue or moss that might affect their champion racer's speed. The season begins with the first snowflakes. As the winter rain thickens, the boys stamp their feet impatiently, climb up to the lan-tern and try to choose the best starting position. They spend hours placing pegs Sevastian has carved from the wood of shipwrecks; on the night in question, they take ages to fall asleep and wake before the sun rises, but then must wait till everyone else is up and Osip has barricaded himself in his office for the games to begin. Outside, a naked Noé ventures from her cabin to feel the first snowfall on her bare shoulders and belly. She's not visible from the bedroom; the tower is dark and already the boys are at the lantern, they've set each stone on its peg, and when finally Mie cries "Ho!" from the back of the cellar, they're entitled to one flick and only one. For ten months, they've been practicing the skill, they've flicked at rocks, trunks, furniture; the younger one has lost a fingernail and the elder's index finger is all calloused. The lighthouse resounds to the clattering of their favourites tumbling down the stairs; Abel yells and his voice ricochets off the walls, the piercing echoes underscoring his excitement. Seth can't keep still, he's capable of racing up and down the five floors twenty times over, nothing tires him out.

After several weeks, the stones lose their attraction, the children grow bored. Mie draws in her notebook, and from time to time changes little Dé, who sleeps on despite his brothers' cries. The boys make armies out of scraps of wood and engage in battle; they conquer the tiles of the floor one by one.

Osip blows on the pale grey wisps of steam rising from his bowl. He drinks through lips pressed together. He's careful not to swallow the leaves that stick to his mouth because he plans to dry them out later and infuse them again: it is tea that gets him through the weeks of north wind. Winters in the lighthouse can drive a person mad. The children, captive in the tower, shout, climb, and invade every space, fiddle with the objects on his desk, pile up coins of foreign currency. Supplies dwindle. The door that looks out onto the world, frozen in ice, creaks but no longer opens.

When there's nothing left to eat but rice, the Old Woman summons her two sons. Sevastian must go out on the hunt again and bring home rabbit or a deer. Osip sounds the foghorn, four blasts ring out – — — —— then waits. Several hours later, Noé appears at the door for a few minutes carrying a torch, a stake, a wooden mallet; she breaks up the ice and melts any fragments that resist, taking care not to damage the hinges, singing as she works. These are the tower's only moments of tranquility: the children glue their ears to the keyhole; they listen to the scraping against the icebound wood, their mother's voice subdues them. When finally the door gives way, they want to throw themselves into her arms but don't dare. There they are, the three of them filling the doorway. Calmly Noé puts away her tools; Sevastian steps over the children's small bodies, walks outside, and closes the door behind him. Before he decamps to the woods, he topples his wife into the snow and takes her right there. The children hear their grunting and sighs, and Osip watches through the spyglass. He wants to grab hold of his penis, but the wind on the gallery is too strong.

The sailors trudge into Seiche and leave deep prints with their wet boots. When they remove them, their toes are swollen and bright red or black and dead, the yellow nails detached; the flesh of their feet is puckered and bulges to their ankles. The cold spreads unimpeded from the sea to the village, it gnaws at men's skin and freezes their eyeballs.

How is it possible, a summer so hot, a winter so cold?

The fog and snow obscure all light for twelve weeks. The silhouettes making their way across the sea look like ghosts rising up from the grey ice all around. As a child, Osip would head down to the docks each year and watch the spectres advance. As the sailors approached, they'd take form: brown faces; thin, flat eyelids; their beards, braided like women's scalps, consuming their cheeks up to the eyes. They reach the banks more dead than alive, their eyelashes rigid with frost, their clothing as stiff as bones.

They don't speak.

They're frightening.

Seiche has two whorehouses and a clandestine bar open twenty weeks a year (twelve in the winter, eight in the summer). Here, in cabins made of barely planed boards, the cargo ship crowd resuscitates. The giants eat little, drink lots; they knock back beer in great gulps, foam trickling down their chins. They wipe their faces with their sleeves, then wring the fabric out over their pint glasses. They are brutes from seedy parts who signed up with the first passing tub; foreign flocks; merchants of tea and spices, lithe and squeaky-clean, standing to drink potato brandy from chipped cups; dice players who ante up worn coins or the beautiful Sabine, come down from the Cité for them.

Once thawed, the seamen tell stories of women and monsters.

Osip listens reverently, hidden between barrels that reek of cheap wine.

Sometimes someone will get up on a table, miming a siren's hips or the attack of an octopus with his hands; he'll raise his shirt and expose his side punctured by a narwhal's tusk. Osip's eyes open wide; he has no idea what a narwhal is, but it must be incredibly fierce to pierce a man as strong as this one.

Age ten, he stays for three days in the stench and the ruckus of the saloon. He doesn't eat, and when it gets too much for him, he shuts his eyes, sleeps standing, propped up by kegs of beer. All around the din continues, only at dawn does the noise abate: it's the silence of the helmsmen slumped over the tables that wakens Osip. He walks among the bodies and takes a closer look at the deformed features, the scars and wounds. Soon he learns to distinguish the scrap dealers from those who transport provisions. The first have deep cuts on their thumb and index finger — actually, it's remarkable they still have all their digits — and the second are always ready to head out; they drink less, tell better tales, their stories evoking countries where cherry blossoms fill trees. As soon as the ice weakens, they'll return to their boat to break up the floes with the hull of their ship and open the way for the others.

On the fourth morning, a tall, slim fellow — his neck long and slender like a woman's, his skin black, his cloak pale grey and lined with fur — springs to his feet as Osip walks by. The boy gives a start and jumps back, then trips over a gruff bear of a man slumped over his pitcher of beer.

— You got somewhere to live?

Osip gives a half-hearted nod.

— Go home.

Osip doesn't move. He looks at the gold jewelry shining around the man's throat, wants to speak, but his lips are thick.

—You're not made for the sea.

Osip rubs his eyes, they're sticky and itchy and he has trouble opening them fully.

—Noise scares you. You'd rather go hungry than steal a piece of bread off a table. Go home.

The man lowers his head. The day before, he'd heard two seamen talk of carting the boy off to their rust bucket once the ice melted.

—You'll starve to death on the ocean.

—I want to see things.

—There's nothing to see. The world's the same wherever you go. Ports, smooth water, rough water, women who'll open up for change and wail when you take your leave. Everywhere the same, I tell you.

Osip doesn't budge. The mariner turns, rummages through a large canvas bag, then holds out a lacquered box embossed in gold.

—This is what I carry on my ship. You, you think it's pretty, mysterious. I've got six hundred others identical to this. When you've seen one, you've seen them all. I'll give it to you if you go home and don't come back.

Osip's heart is pounding in his throat, he feels a sudden rush of heat, and his mouth goes slack as though his tongue has lost its shape. He's never owned anything as precious as this. Gingerly, he takes the box, stares at it a while, then slips it inside his coat,

132

hides it under his sweater. On his way out, he decides to give it to his mother as a present. The eldest has never brought back anything this beautiful for her. But then the idea of parting with the box becomes unbearable and he presses it tighter to his belly. Its texture is cold and smooth. At first, he walks slowly, often turning back to look at the grey wooden cabin; the black man stands in the doorway, isn't going anywhere. At one point he shouts, "Put the leaves in hot water."

Osip hasn't eaten for days. He walks into the house, chews stale bread and collapses beside Leander, who's asleep on the mattress in the little bedroom. The box jabs him in the ribs. He keeps it there.

It's the same box Osip fills every autumn with the leaves Sevastian brings him back from Seiche. Winter passes and the stock of tea dwindles. Come springtime, he must find other sources of pleasure. Reclaiming Noé's body, turned cold and white by the north wind; counting the ships that didn't survive the ice; sounding the horn to scatter the flocks of geese sweeping through the sky.

Once the frost eases, the children go outside. The lighthouse is Osip's again. He spends days alone by his lantern. The spyglass takes the place of his right eye and the sun weathers his face, leaving a pale circle beneath one eyebrow.

He prefers the boys from a distance.

The youngsters have lived one on top of the other for too long. As soon as the Old Woman lets them go, Abel races toward the forest. He's off like a shot the minute the door opens, wanting nothing to do with the beach; he only stops once, in front of Noé's cabin, stands at the foot of the porch — unlike other years, his mother's house is shut tight—and stays put for a moment, wonders if he should knock. In both hands, he's carrying the rabbit snares Sevastian taught him to make during the weeks of cold. Osip observes him from above. The boy sets foot on the first step, changes his mind. He glances over his shoulder, then sprints for the forest again. He finds the hideout under its protective winter layers, pulls away the carefully placed pine boughs and sweeps up the brown needles, then sets his traps, prepares for summer.

Seth, he runs for three days straight. Anywhere, in all directions, only stopping to climb trees or jump into puddles of melted snow. He doesn't share his brother's qualms; he climbs onto the porch, pounds on his mother's door, doesn't wait for an answer, clambers up barrels, hitches himself onto the roof, slides back down the eavestrough, runs a few laps through the forest, then returns to the sea; steps over Dé eating sand, leaps from one rock to the next, doesn't slip on the wet seaweed or slick stones. Later, once he's burned off the winter's excess energy, he drags home branches and bark, begs the Old Woman for wool scraps, then makes miniature boats that he launches onto the waves and watches as they run aground.

Sometimes the cloud cover thickens and turns a dark black, storms a frequent occurrence during spring's high tides. The little ones have to be rounded up inside the tower. Sevastian slings Abel over his shoulder, the boy's forehead banging against his father's back. He's shouting and laughing at the same time; he wanted to watch the storm from his hideout.

All night long, jellyfish are swept up in the breakers. By morning, they lie swollen like blisters on the smooth face of the beach.

Noé half-opens her door. Her head pokes through and the sun strikes her face; she shuts her eyes but keeps her nose in the light, breathes the salt-laden breeze. She stands motionless in the doorway, as if her body craves the shelter inside but her head refuses to return to the lair.

Cautiously, she makes her way outside. She's not ghostly and emaciated like a hibernating animal. She does a full tour to measure the distance that separates her from each of her children. All of them have returned to their respective territories. Mie is the closest at hand, but other than in the evening, she never really comes near. Noé stakes her claim to the beach again, gathers up jellyfish in her pails. Mie makes her own footprints in the sand, walks in her mother's for a while, then drops to the ground. Osip glances at the young girl lying on the beach but turns back to his woman, a giant silhouetted against the mist. Noé bends over. Noé straightens up. Noé gathers medusas the way the Old Woman does mushrooms. The pails bang against her thighs with each step; water runs down her skirt and pastes the fabric to her skin.

Soon enough, she is standing by the steps to the cabin, her enormous buckets filled to overflowing. One moment she's holding a bucket in each hand, in the next they drop; it takes just a few seconds for her knuckles to give way under the weight of the pails that tumble to the ground. There's water everywhere and, lying in the puddles, the indestructible blue spheres and their stinging tangle of tentacles.

Noé stares at her wrists, her fingers, lifts her arms to the light as though they were foreign to her. She turns, looks for something to explain what has just happened. There is no one; Mie is still lying in the waves, Seth's bobbing around near his sister, Abel is off somewhere in the forest. Noé looks at the tipped-over pails and bends to pick up the jellyfish, folding herself into three — her shoulders, her pelvis, her knees — grabs the beasts bare-handed, her skin erupting in red blisters. She's relieved: this pain can't reach her.

She vomits.

Osip is watching from the gallery. He should go down but doesn't budge, paralyzed at the sight of Noé's clumsiness, her erratic movements, and the folly of her grabbing the jellyfish without protecting her fingers.

Once the flaccid bodies have been gathered up, she withdraws inside, shuts the door and goes to ground.

For days, she doesn't resurface.

The black umbra of the ice is imprinted on the sand. The packs have melted, nothing remains but the ashes and dust that hid in their iridescent blue. Among the dead grasses, green spikes are emerging; their stalks quiver with the passing of birds and crabs. Here and there along the shore: traces of the pyre not yet extinguished by the wind. The whale carcass has been eaten by the family and by other passing creatures; slowly the sea washes over its bones and swallows them up one by one.

Osip turns his gaze to the beach. He's seated at the top of the tower with the spyglass around his neck and doesn't know what to focus on. Spectacles such as the flight of white geese in group formation no longer interest him, nor do the tails and the spouting of cetaceans above the waves, the waddling of porcupines descending from the forest at low tide, or the alighting of huge eagles on the lantern before they dive for their prey.

What he really loves is watching Noé watch these same things.

Which leaves Mie. The little girl resembles Sevastian to an unpleasant degree — she has his flat nose, his pale round eyes. Some mornings, she sits herself down on the stairs in the tower and waits for the Old Woman to plait her hair. On these days, she's a blend of her grandmother and her father; at times Osip watches her, unable to imagine what is going through her child's head, wonders what she can be doing as she sits, immobile for hours at a time, amid the cranes of the northern cove or, immobile again, at the mouth of the river. Maybe, like him, Mie is lost. She's used to hanging onto her mother's skirts, only this spring her mother is nowhere to be found.

Osip lets his spyglass wander over the shore. Time devours everything: the days slip by, identical, even the ships leave him cold. He stops comparing the letters on their sides to the markings on the coins he keeps in his desk.

Several times, he heads down and knocks on Noé's door. She doesn't answer. He enters anyway. With each passing year, the cabin fills a little more with disquieting objects he tries not to see. He concentrates on her alone, touches her, lays her down on the bed and wraps himself around her. She must have lived off lard all winter long: her breasts hang heavy on her chest. She surrenders, but with greater resistance. Once he has finished, he no longer tidies the cabin; that has become impossible. He departs, leaving the door open behind him. He wishes that Noé would step outside and give meaning to his days again, but she pulls the sheets around her body, drags her way to the door, and slowly shuts it.

Osip returns to his lighthouse.

As leaves bud, unfurl and turn green in the trees, the ocean changes colour. Grey in winter, it veers to blue, then swells with turquoise and glimmers, darkens to cyan, to ultramarine, and then, in August, shifts to cerulean. Days pass, nothing happens.

One morning, Osip walks into the lighthouse kitchen and finds the eldest's daughter there. She's seated by the table, almost as though she's waiting for him. She sits motionless, her child's hands in her lap and her face, slightly round and slightly angular, calm and serious. When he enters, she murmurs, "Ah." He pauses before her for a moment, then heads over to the hearth, puts water on to boil, pulls roots from a jar that he'll infuse as he waits for teatime. When he turns, Mie is standing so close behind him that he gives a start. Her feral girl's braids haven't been redone for days, and she's crowned with hair run amok. She examines him head to toe, her cheeks red, her body taut, her dress torn at the knees, her legs bitten by flies. She's been twelve for ten days and she says, "I want you to teach me human sex."

He wonders how much courage it must take for the little one to keep looking him in the eye. He wonders if a girl raised in Seiche would have asked such a question and, out of the blue, thinks of the boys wolf-ing down shellfish and sleeping in earthen hideouts.

Mie is twelve.

She is his brother's daughter.

He says, "No."

Then he skirts around her and heads up the tower stairs, tries to climb slowly but all he wants to do is run, to get as far away as possible from her blond aureole and scabbed elbows. He manages to take his time, closes the office door without slamming it, pulls the bolt and then, laying his ear against the keyhole, he listens, strains to hear Mie's steps on the stairs, the distinctive scrape of her heels against stone, the heavy door of the lighthouse opening and closing.

Mie spends the first seven months of her life fastened to her mother's flesh. When the snow melts, Noé uncouples her from her side. She must pry away the fingers Mie wraps around her hair, remove her mouth from her breast and reacquaint her own belly, protected as it has been by the baby's warmth, to the cold of the air. She lays the child in a wicker basket and crosses the spit of sand to the lighthouse. She doesn't enter. She pushes open the door, sets the basket down on the sill and shoves it inside as far as possible. The little one is wrapped in shawls and scarves, her pale curls hidden under a kerchief; she lies for hours in her threadbare swaddling clothes, doesn't cry, doesn't babble. The Old Woman, laden with pine brush and branches, discovers her on her return from the forest.

She trades one load for the other, leaves the brushwood in the entrance, carries the basket up to her son, sets it down in the middle of the kitchen, waits. Brought up short, Osip stares at his niece. She has a fold where her wrists should be, as though her hands were thrust into the end of her arms without taking the time to match one appendage to the other. She breathes green bubbles from her nose. Osip tugs at a corner of his sleeve and wipes her tiny nostrils. He doesn't understand how something so little can be so finely detailed: lips, forehead, ears, almond eyes. The child has her own distinctive traits, a serene, serious face.

He leans over her and she smiles.

He wants to touch her but doesn't know how. For a moment, he holds a tentative hand over the basket, reaches out, then pulls back — not that the baby looks overly fragile — then clasps her belly. The little one slips, but he catches her. Which is when the Old Woman takes the child from him, grabs his wrist, bends his arm, places it against his torso and settles Mie there, her silky skull in the crook of his elbow, his huge man-paw underneath her miniscule knees.

The infant falls asleep with a smile, it drools, a soft rattle to its breath already.

Osip takes over the care of the eldest's child. Every time Sevastian returns from the forest, he snatches her from Osip, cuddles her, this daughter who looks like him, but the minute he tires of her, he lays her back down in the basket or holds her out to his brother. Osip's heart starts beating again.

Often, he takes Mie to the lantern with him. The little one doesn't move around much, just crawls a bit, creeping on all fours and staring at animals. She peers at birds perched on the railing, breaks into laughter when they fly away. If she whimpers, Osip changes her, tickles her ribs with his big finger, and she smiles; when nothing soothes her, he lays the baby on his stomach. His belly is soft, his heart beats slowly; she falls asleep listening to the rumbling against her side. He walks back to his spyglass, to the eldest's woman bathing naked in the waves; the baby is a warm blanket protecting him from the sea's squalls.

"Look here, your woman's with child." The Old Woman is frowning and shaking her grandmother's finger, speaking as though it's plain to see. "Sevastian, find me what I need to knit a new blanket."

Osip is speechless. It never crossed his mind that Noé secreted herself away because she was expecting. With every other pregnancy, she'd kept on with her life till the little ones slid out from between her legs.

"She's twenty-five weeks on," the Old Woman adds.

Osip smiles. Newborns are what he likes best, babies he can hold in his hand, who need nothing but mash and their father's skin.

Osip smiles, his brother calculates.

Twenty-five weeks, that's six months. Sevastian counts back—August, July, June, May, April, March. This is a February baby, conceived in the snow while Osip was watching over the flock in his tower. Over the winter, the younger brother doesn't venture out.

Osip smiles again, obligingly, when Sevastian states, "This child is mine."

Standing in the kitchen, Sevastian has spread the first fall supplies out on the table: a bag of rice, a kilo of sugar, three flasks for the Old Woman, tobacco for Noé, a blank notebook for his daughter. After the first storms, the trail leading to Seiche will be cut off: it always takes him a dozen trips to assemble all the provisions they'll need.

Sevastian empties his pouches, pulling out a new ladle, tea, two kilograms of salt, a glass jar full of yeast, three bags of potatoes. He throws the package of tea leaves over to Osip and repeats, "This child is mine."

To start with: her ankle boots, their leather weathered by time and their soles too heavy. Mie unlaces them the way she would at night, sitting on the end of the mattress. She has hidden her notebook recording her quest beneath it. On the floor are the drawings of the family tree she has made in the dust.

The laces are stiff with dirt and salt. It's always a chore to untie their knots. When the lace gives, crusts of dried mud fall onto the floor and break into sandy crumbs. The Old Woman would tell her to get the broom and sweep it up, but she isn't here, so Mie blows on the dust in order to scatter it more evenly across the floor. Her boots smell of wet leather; she likes the odour, pokes her nose under the tongue, inhales deeply, then throws them by the door. They land in a cloud of grey powder.

Her socks have turned red at the toes and around the heels. The irregularly shaped stains remind her of the maps Noé has drawn in her cabin. Mie takes the socks off one by one, rolling them down from her knees until they form two tight coils at the ends of her feet. She studies her toenails, tries to clean them with her thumb, twists her leg to smell the sole of her foot: not that bad.

She stands up, paces a little around the room. The great heron on the window ledge watches her with a bemused expression. She wishes she knew what order women normally follow when they undress. Might that have been something her great-grandmother taught the Old Woman before she slept with the Old Man? "First your blouse, then your skirt." Or, "First your skirt, then your blouse." What about her underwear? Fold it, lay it out, hide it away?

At night, she usually pulls her clothes over her head and leaves them balled up on the floor till the next day. Everything except her camisole and underpants. She doesn't remember ever being fully naked in the lighthouse. Whenever she changes her underwear, first she puts on a slip, and whenever she changes her dress, she keeps her undergarments on.

She starts by taking off her skirt, folds it once, twice, against herself; the waist shrinks, the sides are still the same length. She lays it over the back of the chair. For the longest time, she stands by the window. They are two—she and the heron—examining her legs, ankle to knee: young maple saplings, as blond and downy as new branches.

Next, she takes off her woolen sweater, which she plans to fold and lay on the rocker over top of the skirt. Osip likes to rearrange Noé's clothes and contemplate their interplay of colours and textures before concentrating on her skin. Mie has constructed an image in her mind: her clothes in a neat pile and her body beneath the sheet. She has imagined Osip discovering her clothing first — fall cotton and red knit — then her. She has convinced herself that the perfect pyramid of her clothes will change the way her uncle views her, but she isn't able to fold her sweater right; it's shrunken and shapeless, its neckline limp, distended under one arm, mended under the other. It doesn't look like anything at all.

The heron keeps jabbing its beak in her direction then turning back to the sea. Mie imagines it's making fun of her, or that maybe it wants to help. She asks, "Are you laughing at me?" and the bird shuts its eyes, stretches its wings even more.

Eventually, she rolls up the sweater in the bottom of a trunk and glances at the skirt — she likes it, at least — laid carefully over the back of the chair. She likes the way the grime fades from the hem to the waist. The fade in the fabric seems deliberate, so much has the dirt been absorbed by the cotton.

Wool underpants cover her thighs to the knee. The tail of her blouse hides a bit of her behind and the elastic in her skirt has left a mark around her waist. She has grown a lot this summer — her blouse gapes between the buttons. She has trouble undoing them without tearing the fabric, has to pull the sides together, suck in her belly and push each button through its hole.

Folding her blouse is easier. She smooths the collar down and makes sure it can be seen from the doorway.

Suddenly, she's worried Osip will prefer the smell of Noé's dresses to this tidy pile. She has often seen him plunge his nose into her mother's clothes. She leans over her own that smell of nothing but wind and skin. She opens the Old Woman's trunk, rummages among the scarves and shawls and finds, rolled up in a grey silk square, the pink perfume bottle she has seen her use from time to time. Carefully, she unwraps it, scrutinizes the vial, touches the atomizer — a long tassel of black thread hangs from the end of the spray pump. She pulls the pile of clothing over and gently presses down on the pump. Its fragrant mist shimmers like noon snow and then disappears, absorbed by the fabric. Mie buries her nose in the clothes. The perfume's fragrance must have diminished with time. She pumps again, once, twice. Then stops, afraid the Old Woman will notice.

She wanders around in her camisole and underpants. Other than as a distorted reflection in rippling ponds, she has never seen herself from head to toe. She doesn't know how her body looks and believes it to be more like Noé's than it actually is. She's aware that she's not as tall and is slightly broader than her mother, but can't quite manage to superimpose these differences on Noé's appearance.

She approaches the window opening onto the sea. Red and grey ships pass close to the lighthouse and salute her uncle with a blast of their foghorns. She has never thought of him as a man of importance before. And yet he must be if these people from afar interrupt their routine to send him greetings.

The scent of the perfume makes her head ache.

She can't bring herself to shed the camisole. She sifts through the summer linens to find the diaphanous fabric she thought she'd cover herself with, then stretches out on the mattress, envelops herself in the translucent material and only then decides to remove the yellowed top that hides her body. Wrapped in gossamer, she gauges the transparency of the fabric by checking to see if the brownish circles of her breasts, her navel, and the hair below show through.

The heron has slid its head under one wing, whereas she, enveloped in the gauzy linen, keeps her eyes wide open.

Mie pushes on the door without knocking and enters the cabin like the wind. This is the first time she has ever set foot inside. She had bounded up from the shore, along the small path and up the stairs and— not even winded—onto the porch. She imagines herself to be the mist, the breeze, something free to roam anywhere without permission—and turns the doorknob. Then, as though this was nothing out of the ordinary, she gives the door a shove. It groans on its hinges and she walks over to the table made of planed planks of wood in the middle of the room. Only then does she come to a stop.

Now Mie is no longer a gust of wind, or a wisp of fog; she is herself standing in her mother's lair.

At first she sees nothing. She smells the aroma of dried herbs, flowers, glue, mushrooms, and skins. Then her eyes become used to the half-light and she sees grey walls covered in drawings that have crumbled into dust, been washed out by water seepage, redrawn and moisture-stained once more. She immediately

recognizes the sea, its flow and its meanders travers-
ing the boards. She recognizes the forest, the clear-
ings, and the paths to the cliffs, sees the trails taken
by Sevastian and the brothers' hideout, the hollows in
the sand, the caves. A bed is propped against the wall.
All paths are born here: the mattress is the cabin, the
centre of the world.

The room is peopled with strange shadowy figures
whose pupils, black as marbles, are turned on Mie. She
furrows her brow and squints, tries to make out the
monsters that share this lair. Slowly, they materialize:
a half-dozen animals that seem to be alive but are well
and truly dead. The creatures don't frighten her. In one
way or another, they are an extension of her mother.
Even before she discerns them, Mie has fallen in love.

A fawn with giant bat wings outstretched on either
side of its spine. The head, then torso, of a grey wolf
that ends in a seal's tail. The velvety antlers of a rabbit.
The head of a buffalo adorned with crow feathers. A
goose with the muzzle of a fox.

Mie draws closer, leans over an otter-salmon, lightly
touches the barely perceptible seam between the two
hides, one hairy, one covered in scales. The animal
seems real. What kind of gaze does it level on the
world? What would she see through its eyes? A string
is tied to the end of its fin. Mie pinches it between her
fingers and follows it to the wall. The string is fastened

to a specific spot in the picture—a whitish atoll in the dark of the sea. After a while, accustomed to the half-darkness, she sees every strand linking the other beasts to pins on the walls. Seven creatures attached to as many islands.

In the centre, Noé reigns over them all.

If she looked up when she heard the little one enter, there's no knowing now. Her neck strains toward her work, her forehead is bent over her hands. She is humming softly. She's ensconced in an armchair, the springs of which offer no support, the seat hollow beneath her bottom. She's busy sewing the spotted wings of an owl to the pelt of a hedgehog. Beside her, set out on a worn velvet cushion, are a squirrel's tail and two pieces of polished jade. Once stuffed, the creature will fit in the palm of her hand.

Mie could never have conceived of so many curious objects gathered together in a single place. Jars of earth, bones, skulls; a ball that looks like the Old Woman's skeins of wool but which is wrapped in thin, milky threads of spiders' webs; canning jars; all sorts of herb bouquets hung by their roots; knives, wicker bags, oxidized copper pots and pans; hides stretched over windows and nailed to the floor; stars painted on the ceiling; misshapen pebbles and rocks; a teapot, two crystal glasses; straw and twig bundles; bowls of pine cones; an ivory pipe, jewelry, candles.

She lingers, looks around. She walks over to the fawn, touches its muzzle, the white insides of its ears. Its eyelashes quiver when she breathes on them. Its eyes are huge. Mie stares at the two black beads, imagines that this deer can also scrunch up its mind, plunge it into the skull of a human, and see the world through other eyes. The fawn's bat wings are unfurled on either side of its spine, broad and powerful. Mie puts her hand on the membrane, then glides her finger to the claw of its thumb. She likes this animal, at once gentle and fierce, fragile on its skinny legs, strong with its open wings. Noé might have said, "It's you," though if she did she murmured the words so softly it all seems like a dream. But Mie looks at the fawn and knows. "It's me."

Three more beasts are her brothers. She recognizes them, and Osip and Sevastian too. The Old Woman must be the fox with a goose's body.

It takes a long time before Mie remembers the reason for her visit — she's transfixed by Noé's precision, by her ability to comprehend the essence of her children despite not being familiar with their deeds, their strange habits, their voices, because she has hardly touched them at all, has not felt the way their hearts beat beneath their skin. But at last Mie steps closer to her mother, stands before her and says, "I asked Osip to take me like a woman."

Noé's fingers halt in mid-flight, her needle and thread like white fissures splitting the air. Mie thinks her hand beautiful, she likes the way its ring finger avoids touching the hide, its nails pink under the grime, the wrinkles on her knuckles accentuated by dust. Noé unkempt and full of grace.

—I asked Osip to take me like a woman.

Her mother raises her head. She says nothing, doesn't look at Mie. She stares at the door open onto the beach and the sea. Her cheeks flush. Mie watches as they redden in the light streaming inside. Its radiance is carved into rectangles along the dark wall. Mie waits. The words need to find a way through the creatures, songs, and ocean maps. The path is long, the words need time. She stays put, her eyes as large as the fawn's.

Finally, Noé inhales, draws the bottomless breath of an animal that is assumed to be dead but suddenly decides to breathe again. She speaks.

"You have to put jellyfish in a pit after a storm, otherwise the waves come back for them and flood the cabin."

Mie wishes she had a response. Words bump up against her lips, she doesn't know what to say, so she follows up with her other sentence.

"Maybe that way he'll leave you alone."

Noé hears, or perhaps she does not. She says, "If

you want to spool spider webs, then you have to wait for dusk."

Mie brings her fingers to her mother's face, to her mottled features, her soft hair, brown, auburn, and white. Noé is like the stuffed animals, her eyes two black and piercing beads unwavering in the dark, her ankles sturdy despite their slimness, her skin pocked like a fish's, strength in her neck, breast, and shoulders. She doesn't react. Mie touches her cheek.

"You must leave at least the length of an arm between a fire and the cauldron or the lard will burn instead of melting."

The little one stays still. Her fingers begin to tingle as if medusas were living beneath her mother's skin. Her mother's jaw clenches against her palm. Noé says, "Wash the bones. Always wash the bones with river water and salt," then returns to her work. Mie is sure she's creating the animal that will depict the child she's carrying. A hedgehog-owl with a squirrel's tail. She senses it will be a girl. Silent joy brings a rush of warmth. She'd like to know whether, before she was born, her mother created the fawn in the same way. How does she know the temperament of a baby before it is even thrust into the world? Or is she the one who creates it? She sews the wings onto the prickly fur, her awl piercing the skin, the thread disappearing between the quills. This beast is quite unlike the fawn; its feathers are folded against its side and purely decorative, the possibility of flight aborted.

Mie is mesmerized by the silver flash of the needle in the darkness of the cabin. She watches her mother steady her arm against her belly and sew. Mie sits on a corner of the table, her feet dangling, slivers of wood piercing her thighs.

She breathes and her ribs open, a long, slow intake of air. She exhales, her torso stiffens and hollows out, her skeleton lengthens as do her spine and her head.

She tries something new. In the same way she became the bear, the otter, the crane, the crab, she becomes the cabin.

She feels between her walls the wild pulsating of her mother's blood. A force, contained by partitions, that spills toward the ceiling, the door, and would break the windows and whip like a storm along the beach and as far as the lighthouse were it not kept in check. Its power is staggering to Mie, totally unanticipated. In taking on the spirit of the house, she thought she would grasp the life of its boards, the work of humidity on its wood, the mould eating away at the frame, the wind in the curtains, and just maybe, with a bit of luck, she would be able to tap into a little of Noé, see the traces of Osip's visits, gain insight into their encounters. But her mother fills and overflows this space. Noé is the one securing the stones, making the glass tremble, distending the cushions' fabric, swelling the doors. The cabin stays standing through her will alone.

Mie would like to focus on the objects. Contemplate them one by one, analyze the drawings on the walls, tame the spirit of the stuffed creatures, guess at what lies hidden in the urns and jars. But she can't. Blood pounds in her ears, her throat tightens, a shiver courses through her arms from scapula to shoulder to elbow — something is crushing her ribs and her lungs. She has trouble breathing, collapses.

This cabin will not be observed.

The floor is covered in sand. This is the first thing she notices when she opens her eyes. The rough texture against her face. And then, she hears her. Noé, singing. Mie lies for eons on the ground, swaddled in her mother's voice uniting the two of them, her future hedgehog sister and her, in the cabin returned to stillness.

Along the dock, tall vessels
In sea swells silently tilting
Fail to guard against cradles
That women insist on rocking.

Ensconced in the bed in the lighthouse, Mie tries
to remember the rest of the words her mother sang
in the cabin, but she can't. She does remember lying
there for a long time, slumped in front of the goose
with a fox's head, able to drag herself from the room
only once Noé too had left it to watch the sun drop
into the waves. She'd started by crouching under the
table, her mother silhouetted against the light in the
doorway — her skirts, her hair, her arms long and
lithe like rope, her fingers skinny cords knotted at
their ends. Mie glanced at the objects piled up on the
shelf across from her and spotted a long, flat, narrow
container. Staying low to the floor, she drew near,
grabbed it, and slid it into her smock. Even though it
was made of wood, the tobacco box kept clinking like

metal; she went out the back way and, leaning against the wall of the cabin, opened the box—the small hinged lid inlaid with ivory and jade—and tipped its contents into her lap. A white feather, a copper sphere attached to a lock of black hair, a desiccated queen bee carefully wrapped in a piece of black fur. She didn't have time to grasp the meaning of her discovery; the bushes shook and she stuffed everything into her pockets. Abel appeared and rushed over, wanted to know what she'd found in the house. He followed her to the beach, saying over and over, "Tell me."

Picture our forest. See it stretching into the distance, farther than you can walk in a month's time. Imagine the trees Sevastian has never seen, so remote are they, beyond mountains, beyond rivers, beyond lakes we know nothing of, their water as clear as that of the lagoons. It's our forest, but it is infinite. The clearing is golden and grey. The ferns are autumn red. Leaves drop onto rocks. A brook cuts the clearing in two; its current has eaten the soil away. A pond lies in the shelter of a pine tree.

Watch the black stag, his muzzle deep in the water. Have you seen how his hide is like the night? You have never encountered an animal like this, with antlers so tall and fur so dark. He is the only one of his kind, he lives deep in the forest where no one ventures but other beasts.

He is our grandfather.

He drinks. Look through his eyes. Do you see the glimmer of sunlight in the pond? Does the light remind you of the flame of a candle reflected in a window? It is dusk. Our grandmother paddles, her white wings like winter snow. There are no other swans in the forest. The crows say she fled from a castle's pond and followed the twists and turns of the creek to the clearing here. When Grandfather Stag catches sight of her, the sun's rays strike her plumage and she is sequined in gold.

This is the story of a black stag and a swan who love one another, give birth to a daughter, and are devoured by wolves. The wolf pack raises the child until she falls into the river and is swept away to the sea, where she is taken in by a whale, who carries her on its back to humankind's shore. Mie invents the story as she goes, picking up the objects around her that serve as her inspiration: the white feather she found in the tobacco box, branches like antlers spat out by the waves, a stone in the shape of a fish. She doesn't want to talk about the creatures she discovered in the cabin, so she imagines something slightly different, better. As Abel showers her with questions, she sits on a dead tree trunk the sea deposited overnight, smoothed and burnished by salt and sand. She says,

"This is the story of Noé." And adds, "This is the story of where we come from." Now she tells the tale.

Grandmother Swan wraps her neck around Grandfather's rack. With her beak, she caresses the black coat no one has seen on any other stag. Can you feel the soft caress of her feathers along the dark male's fur? Their manner of loving is like nothing else in the forest.

Mie doesn't speak quickly, often she coughs. Her eyes pass from one brother to the other; she holds herself tall, turns her head this way and that, her hair a tempest around her scalp, her brow furrowing and smoothing out incessantly. Then she rises to her feet, sticks two branches in her headband, and walks as she always has, a little awkwardly and without grace. She has put her arms out in front of her belly, bends over and circles around the boys, swaying left then right; she's a big, clumsy stag clasping the white feather, she brushes her brothers' faces with its barbs.

The sun begins its descent, turning both the beach and the children's blond hair red.

Wolves have clamped onto Grandmother Swan's throat and decapitated her. Imagine the pleasure of fangs sinking into tender flesh. They shake her long white gullet, her beak striking the air then their flanks again and again; they let the blood run across their tongues and drip onto the snow. Her final shreds of skin tear away. To one side are her skull and half of her neck, to the other, her body. Her legs are slack, her outstretched wings have fallen back against her sides. All of Grandmother lies splattered on the ground. Can you feel the shiver of joy coursing through the pack? Imagine the pleasure of this warm soup in winter. Imagine the pleasure of pulsing entrails swelling with the fat they need to confront the cold. The pack devours her breast and her belly. It is beneath her carcass that they find the little girl, covered in blood and feathers. They eat her mother greedily and the stag, her father, his eye sockets empty and his viscera scattered across the clearing, lies a few metres away.

Mie tells her tale. Abel plays with a stick and a length of rope. His fingers keep busy; he's not watching what he's doing, all his attention is focused on his sister's voice and her bizarre dance. In the meantime, his hands make a fishing net all on their own. Seth's legs are crossed, right foot under his left thigh, left foot under his right. His splayed knees tap against the ground, but otherwise he is calm. At one point, Noé passes close to the two of them, a large grey phantom against the open sea. She has covered her shoulders with the skin of a deer, her hair tumbles down her back, her heels sink into the sand. She disappears into the dunes beyond the trees by the cliffs.

The she-wolf steps forward to take a bite of the child. The little one stares at her without blinking. She doesn't cry. She is enveloped in her mother's wing, naked against the soft, spattered feathers.

Some time later, Sevastian appears along another path that leads from the lighthouse to the forest. On his back: an empty pouch, a metal bow. Mie likes his woodman's shoulders. He waves at them before vanishing between the trees.

If you are the whale, you feel a tiny little something tickling you. Imagine an ant on your leg, a button falling onto your belly. The little girl is no bigger than a stray pebble when she hits the flukes of your tail. The whale turns its pupil toward the something; she floats among the seaweed, she is blue and white.

Finally, it's Osip who makes his way down. He hesitates on the path. Mie thinks he'll follow Noé to the cove, he only ever steps onto the beach for her. But he stays where he is, paces behind the young brothers, never coming to a stop, his footprints endlessly erased by the waves. He doesn't come close enough to hear the story, but instead observes from afar. Mie keeps seeing him in the periphery of her gaze, the face of a man staring at her, and suddenly she begins to quake, her story unravels, the boys don't listen quite as hard.

She walks through cities full of shadows. She could have made out people in the play of light, but she sees nothing but obstacles. She is the daughter of a stag and a swan. The movement of her feet is a dance to avoid colliding with humans. There are white fountains and pink stones, houses taller than the cabin, as big as the lighthouse, arrows pointing to the sky, long grey shapes that evoke the sea. Forests are caged in by stakes.

A blast of wind from offshore bears the white feather aloft and carries it away. Abel, Seth, Mie: all three look up, follow it as it swirls out to the sea and, as Abel rushes into the water to retrieve it, Osip gathers the courage to move in closer. He pulls Mie by the arm, says nothing at first and then blurts out, "Okay you know the thing you asked me for the other day in the kitchen I'll show you tomorrow after the noon ships."

Every sound suggests the tapping of heels on the stone of the staircase.

Not one is a footstep.

Mie waits in her bed.

She stares at the heron unfurling its wings on the window ledge. Beneath the sheet, she discovers the nakedness of her legs rubbing against each other, the soft, pale down of her calves, the rough skin on either side of her knees. Cold palms on warm thighs.

She is familiar with her body when it is clothed. She has probed it beneath her garments and woolens; she has explored it despite the impediment of underwear (her hand blocked by the seam in her underpants, harsh fabric against her knuckles). She knows her lips and their flower shape, the slit as hollow as a swamp — when she inserts her fingers, they're drawn further inside, like a foot sinking into mud that must then be tugged out — and the crack between her cheeks less moist than the rest, and the tangle of hairs. What she discovers, as she lies naked under the sheets, is the smallness of her body in the space of the room.

She could leave. Join her brothers out hunting in the woods.

The bird kicks against the window jamb.

She dreams of living in the cabin, of making its treasures, windows, and ceiling her own. She wants the house to give itself up to her. The next time she sets foot inside, she will be a woman. Its walls will no longer resist her.

Mie has found the words to use with Noé when next she confronts her. She repeats them several times over, speaking softly so that Osip won't hear.

—I know that you are bigger than Sitjaq.

Facing the sea, the heron is about to soar away.

—You are bigger than Sitjaq.

She crumples up her being, clicks her tongue against the roof of her mouth, and takes flight with the heron.

VII

Noon's shafts of light spill through the window. Osip's thoughts have turned to the ephemera that gather in black columns on the shore come spring. Steam rises from his cup of tea the way the insects do from the ground. Ships cleave the waves and infiltrate the bay. He's not watching the procession of red and white ships keeping time, daubs against the blue of sea and sky. He stays seated at the table his father made, takes tiny sips of tea. The leaves adhere to the rim of the cup; when they stick to his lips, he spits them out.

How long will Sevastian be gone? He said he was heading for the mountains by Circé. A four-day walk to fetch the sweet beans the boys so love. The Old Woman uses them to buy herself peace and quiet in the winter when nothing else works.

His first infusion of the fall. He drinks, turning the cup slowly in the palm of his hand. As it empties, the leaves adhere to the porcelain and soon nothing is left but their black pattern. Osip sighs. Sevastian told him some women can read the future simply by looking at the image created there.

Mie is waiting for him. At first, he thought she wouldn't come, but before the tide nibbled away at the path, he saw her leave the forest and cross the spit of land below. For the past two hours, she has been downstairs in the deserted bedroom. He has waited a good while to see if she would leave. She has stayed.

Dé is with the Old Woman picking mushrooms in the clearing. Abel is doing the rounds of the snares he has set in the forest. Seth is playing with a boat he must have built during the summer. The path will soon be entirely swallowed up by the sea: no one will be able to come or go from the lighthouse till mid-afternoon.

The drying leaves have settled in the shape of a cauldron, maybe an octopus, Osip can't decide which. He dips his finger into the cup, touches the leaves, swirls them about, but not too much. He'd like to tweak the pattern slightly, change his life by moving a few specks around the bottom of a cup.

A ship blows its horn. Not a warning—a greeting. Osip doesn't climb up to the gallery to reply. If he did, he'd be tempted to pick up the spyglass and train it on Noé's cabin. And if he sees Noé, he won't go down to Mie.

More than anything, he wishes the bottom of his cup would tell a story other than his own.

He gets up, and in doing so scrapes the chair along the floor so that the little one in the room below will be sure to hear him, then walks out of the office. On the threshold, he hesitates — the bedroom, or the lookout? He places one foot on the first step and pauses, his life may be at stake, then at last, he turns his back to the lantern, his heavy shoes sounding on the stone. He grips the railing as he descends.

VIII

Mie is asleep. She dreams of eels turning into ropes becoming snakes, bolting to the sea to escape her fingers. The creatures writhe across the waves, she runs after them, they mustn't disappear. She dives and water closes over her, soon she is fully immersed, the waves' roiling rocks her and pulls her gently to the bottom.

Her dreams always end the same way. She drowns. Both in the dream and in her bed, she has stopped breathing. Then her skin begins to burn, it feels like she's being boiled alive when suddenly she emerges from her slumber as if from the swell. She snaps up to a seated position, takes in great gulps of air. Cold burns her throat and grips her lungs.

Osip is coming down the stairs.

The echo of his footsteps resounds throughout the tower. His heel strikes the stairs and three other heels respond—it's as though an army of men is advancing on her room.

Mie trembles a little as she tries to rearrange her body under her veil. She no longer remembers what the precise positioning of her hands and torso should be. She recalls having pointed her toes to make her sturdy child's legs look longer, but nothing more. And so, her calves look slim and her ankles slender, but she can only improvise from her hips to her head. She shivers, her heart has got to stop palpitating like the wings of an ailing butterfly, she won't be alluring if she coughs and twitches.

Osip has stopped on the landing. She imagines his thick silhouette on the other side of the door, his hand suspended in the air, his fingers hesitating on the doorknob. His sleeves rub against his belly — a rustling like paper that reverberates against the walls — and he raises his fingertips to his chin, the skin blue and stubbly; maybe he should have shaved, he doesn't know.

Mie's breathing grows quiet. Along the window frame, a spider has spun its web and caught a bee. Mie tips her head back to see the captive better. Its yellow and black are now grey with filament. Mie never borrows the body of beasts about to perish, but they fascinate her all the same. She listens to the last traces of sound, the aborted intake of breath. The bee doesn't die straight away, but soon it ceases its vain struggle. Mie finds it beautiful even from a distance; she has observed insects up so close that she can imagine the details that cannot be seen from the bed: the bee's hind legs, the baskets of pollen in perfumed cushions against its belly, its proboscis, its antennae.

She thinks of Seth, who loves honey the way the Old Woman does liquor. She thinks of the desiccated bee she found in the tobacco box. A queen. When Noé smokes the bees out from the hives and gathers the jelly in matte clay jars, she sings—

The bee softly buzzes
Laying eggs so round,
To the larvae, her children,
She sings from the swarm.

Quick, quick, little queens
Grow your iridescent wings
So mine in turn can sweep me
Aloft into the forest of trees.

Mie closes her eyes. She did once borrow the body of a queen bee. Surrounded by the swarm, she abandoned a hive full of worker bees because a new monarch was about to hatch among the cells. She gave up the nest that had become too small, too crowded, and left with half the colony to settle elsewhere. It made Mie think of her mother, a layer of eggs bearing children she ignored. From the big lighthouse mattress, she remembers the flight of the swarm. Half of her little ones buzzed around her—a continuous, protective song—as she abandoned her home and left a newborn daughter with the hive and the other half of her offspring.

"You are bigger than Sitjaq."

Something shifts.

Osip still hesitates on the landing. A southerly wind traverses the sheet. The bee breaks out of the web, its wings thrumming, and the spider falls and slips behind a piece of furniture. The escapee flits aimlessly for a while, then disappears through the window.

Mie feels her heart drop into her stomach. She keeps lying there, hasn't budged; other than the fugitive pollen-gatherer, nothing in the room has changed.

Noé, the daughter of a swan and a stag, is a snow-white doe, a buzzard, a salamander, a wolf, a siren, a whale.

Noé is a queen of bees.

The kind of queen who leaves without waiting to see whether the new sovereign will be strong enough to take her place.

Noé has drawn all the trails of the forest, using charcoal for the ones the boys take, red clay for Sevastian's paths, and nothing but water warping the walls for several other translucent routes Mie does not recognize. Noé says, "You must put jellyfish in a pit..." when Mie tells her "I asked Osip to take me like a woman."

Noé dictates the laws of nature and those of the cabin.

The little one wishes she could remember all the maps drawn on walls, but all she remembers are their filmy blisters.

She tries to calculate the distance her mother might have already travelled, despite her belly and her baggage.

All at once, she's afraid. Will she be able to master the cabin on her own, hold it up on its soft foundation of stones?

Behind the door, Osip must have regained his composure. He lays his clammy hand on the doorknob and slowly turns the handle.

Lying in her woman's pose, Mie speaks out loud so that the word resounds against the walls and inside her head, "*Gone.*"

The door opens: a raspy creaking that takes on a deeper timbre.

She's gone.

ACKNOWLEDGEMENTS

Thank you to Pierre Leroy and the
Fondation Jean-Luc Lagardère.
Thank you to Murielle Mayette and the
Académie de France in Rome.

Thank you to Lise Bergevin, Chloé Deschamps,
Pierre Filion and Isabelle Jubinville.
Thank you to Susan Ouriou for her loving
and attentive translation.
Thank you to Noah Richler for his
enthusiasm and trust.
Thank you to Maria Golikova, Cindy Ma,
Alysia Shewchuk, and the rest of the team
at Arachnide.
Thank you to Salmé Genest-Brissette.
And above all, thank you to Pascal Brissette.

The translator also expresses her gratitude
to the author, Noah Richler, and Barbara Scott.

The author benefited from the support of the
Canada Council for the Arts
while writing this novel.

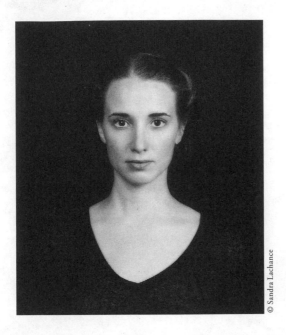

AUDRÉE WILHELMY was born in 1985 in Cap Rouge, Quebec, and now lives in Montreal. She is the winner of France's Sade Award and a finalist for the 2019 Prix du Roman d'Ecologie. She has been a finalist for the Governor General's Literary Award, the Prix France-Québec, and the Quebec Booksellers Award. *The Body of the Beasts* is her third novel and the first to be translated into English.

SUSAN OURIOU is an award-winning writer, editor, and literary translator with over thirty translations and co-translations of fiction, nonfiction, children's, and young adult literature to her credit. She has won the Governor General's Literary Award for Translation. She also recently published *Nathan*, a novel for young readers. Susan Ouriou lives in Calgary.